Ivy Jones' Incredible Adventure

Ivy Jones' Incredible Adventure

JOLENE ROSE

Thriller Publishing Group, Inc.

Ivy Jones' Incredible Adventure

Thriller Publishing Group, Inc.

Copyright©2022JoleneRose

ISBN 978-1-954518-11-7 (Paperback)

ACKNOWLEDGEMENTS

Thanks to the many wonderful people who supported me in the writing of my first book!

One
Don't look

Eighteen-year-old Ivy Jones had long, dark hair and a dainty nose. Her face was round and small. She had a slim body and was tall for her age. She had just moved into a new house in England because her parents had just divorced. She never wanted to move away from her dad but sometimes things like that happen.

On the outside of her new house were columns and arched windows twenty feet high. The house may have once been nice; it might have been the home of an actual family. But scrub and tall weeds now covered the yellow lawn, which clearly hadn't been cut in years. A wire fence boarded the property, sagging at spots wind had knocked it down, a wooden gate hanging from its post. The house was an old brown wreck, its clapboard weathered and cracked, several roof shingles missing. Ivy was disappointed by the fact that instead of a nice, big, clean house as promised, she got a dirty, ugly, and unwelcoming one. She slowly stepped toward the door, twisting the door knob slowly.

Ivy waltzed in the door and was astonished by what she saw next. Polished wood floors and a graceful banister that curved up toward a soaring second floor gallery. The walls were bumpy. Almost like popcorn walls, but rougher. Velvet drapes framed the windows, the lace inner curtains remained drawn, allowing daylight to enter while rendering the heart-stopping view over the city a blur. Ivy ran upstairs the spiraling staircase.

A couple weeks later, Ivy, her stepfather, and her mom finally got all of their stuff unpacked. Her room was small with clean white walls, a twin size bed, a desk with a blank blotter on it, sliding closets opposite the bed, and thin green shag rug at the foot of the bed. A computer faced the window. Occasionally a bird or plane flew by in the distance.

Ivy had decided to invite a friend over. Her name was Madison Rogers. She had thick, blonde hair, rosy cheeks and a sharp jawline. She was just a year older than Ivy–which made her nineteen. The two excited girls jumped and squealed as they hadn't seen each other in quite a while. The girls had been friends since they were toddlers. They lived next to each other and played almost every day. The girls sprinted outside into the backyard. The grass was especially high and thick. It was a rich green and almost soft. The girls tumbled in the grass and laughed. "I bet I could roll down this hill and beat you." Ivy teased.

"Impossible." Madison giggled. The girls rolled down the hill when they noticed a shed. It was mysterious and felt eerie.

Ivy noticed a step leading to a window. She tripped on it but eventually made her way onto it.

Madison peered into the unordinary window next to Ivy that had wide eyes and raised eyebrows. "What is it?" Madison asked, eager.

"You don't want to know, '' Ivy whispered, eyes still as wide as saucers.

"Yes, yes I do!"

Ivy was frozen with fear. Her arms were glued to her sides and her legs were stiff.

Madison was looking at her from a distance but then began jogging to her statue-like body. Madison shoved Ivy out of the way and trampled onto the step, eager to see what was inside. She shook with fear after peeking inside the mysterious window. Both girls, frozen. Not because they were cold, but because of the unusual business in the shed. The two curious girls shuffled sideways toward the door. The girls took deep breaths and closed their eyes, preparing themselves for what they were about to encounter.

Just when Ivy and Madison were turning the door knob, the girls heard Ivy's mom holler, "grab the dog!" The backyard at the old house was fenced in. Apparently, Ivy's mom was still used to that and let the dog out in the non-fenced backyard. The girls flinched and sprinted for the dog. The dog's name was Ozzy. Ozzy was a brown dog and had white hairs around his muzzle as he was getting old. 9 years already. Ozzy's legs have gone stiff because he was getting so old. That's why the girls were surprised when he sprinted out the door. The only reason Ozzy stopped was to examine the shed. He seemed to find it unusual. Ozzy sniffed and sniffed, scratching at the door, barking at the windows, and trying to get up the stairs. Ozzy never had much of a habit to bark, but when he did, something wasn't right. Ozzy then began barking, whining, howling, and growling at the door. The girls got startled and ran inside. For some reason the dog didn't follow. Madison and Ivy couldn't care less about leaving Ozzy behind. They were terrified, overwhelmed, tense, and frightened by the scene the dog had caused.

When it was time for Madison to go, she yanked her bag off the hook beside the front door and said her goodbyes-not forever of course.

The next day, Ivy woke up and immediately opened her curtains, gazing at the shed, pondering whether or not she should go in. Ivy got dressed and ran downstairs, holding both her tennis shoes by her two first fingers and then glancing over at the breakfast table and taking a single bite of some toast before jolting out the back door to open the shed.

Ivy sprinted across the yard, still chewing her toast and all. She then proceeded to study that thing again.

Almost a fuzzy, pink thing with occasional purple sparks flying out of it. Although she still couldn't see what it was exactly. She did notice that every once-in-awhile the thing would change to blue. Or sometimes the shed would shake like someone was yelling or screaming of happiness. "Surely nobody could be yelling or screaming in anger. I mean c'mon it's a pink...hole? I don't know." Ivy whispered to herself. She connected her forehead to the window. Itching to go in.

She slowly stepped toward the door and put

her small hand on the cold, copper door knob. Slowly twisting it, Ivy hesitated "Maybe I should wait for Madison." She spoke softly to herself. "Oh, but I really want to go in," Ivy groaned. "Maybe just a peek." Ivy's excitement grew larger and larger as she began twisting the door knob.

"Hey!" Ivy's step dad shouted. His name is Al. Al angrily walked over to Ivy and shouted "What are you doing over here?"

Ivy quickly stepped off of the stairs leading up to the door and told her step dad all about the enchanting yet unusual thing in the shed. "And there are sparks that come out of it and– and–" Al cut her off.

"Well why don't you just walk in and see what happens?"

"I want to wait for Madison." Ivy replied.

"Okay suits yourself." Al spoke, twisting the door knob all the way and purposely falling into the shed. Ivy stopped walking and turned around to peek at what was inside. "Honey, there's nothing in here." Al said, confused. Ivy was extremely confused and disappointed.

Madison suddenly came running out the back door. Ivy turned toward her and they hugged. Ivy explained what was going on and silence filled the backyard with confusion. "Dad I swear there was a huge, uh glowing and, um magnificent, yeah magnificent, oh I don't know what to call it." Ivy stuttered.

A blank stare appeared on Al's face "Haha. That was a good prank Ivy. Almost better than the ghost prank you did to me last week!" Al chuckled and went inside.

"Well I guess he doesn't have to believe us," Madison tried to lighten the mood. "I mean, we see it so who cares if he does?"

"I guess you're right. Let's try to go in now." Ivy spoke. The two girls decided it was time to go in.

As the girls fearfully walked towards the door, they heard a voice. It was disembodied but breathy. It sounded as if someone was talking out of the sky. "What the-"

Ivy cut Madison off by placing her hand over her mouth tightly. "I've read about this before." Ivy whispered, being as quiet as she possibly could be. "These two girls were walking in a forest and heard a voice just like this. Nobody knows what happened next. Rumor– has it that they were kidnapped." Her voice shook and she looked around, alert for whatever may happen next.

Madison yanked her hand off of her mouth and glanced at Ivy. "That's bull crap." Ivy gasped. "Yeah, I said it. I'll say it again. Bull crap." Madison spoke mockingly.

"It is not. It's true." Ivy snarled, crossing her arms and standing straight up, trying to be taller than Madison. "Whatever, let's just see what's inside."

The girls walked towards the shed, shaking with fear. Madison moved the door knob slowly and opened the door. It creaked and Madison let go of it, letting the door hit the wooden wall. Both Madison and Ivy stood at the doorway, frozen with confusion. The enchanting thing wasn't there anymore. "How is it not there anymore? It was here before my dad showed up. I thought we could see it? Why is it gone? Did we do something wrong?" Ivy sounded desperate and upset.

"Okay calm down. Everything will be okay. Let's try to close the door and open it back up again. That's what they do in movies isn't it?" Madison suggested.

"You're right. Close it." Ivy replied.

Just as Madison was turning the door knob, Ivy spoke yet again. "Wait," Ivy trembled. "What about the voice?"

"Ivy, get over yourself. There is no voice!" But Madison definitely raised hers at Ivy.

"But think about it. I've heard that voice everywhere. My dreams, at school," Ivy started talking fast and began pacing. "Oh, and we can't forget when I'm studying, and even over the Intercom at school and-" Madison broke her word off as Ivy grew angry.

"Will you just shut up about the voice already? It wasn't even clear what it said. It was just mumbling and nonsense. Plus, I am trying to see what is behind this magic door and there have been way too many interruptions. Just stop talking about it already because I am so over it." Madison practically screamed in Ivy's face as she also grew with anger.

"Fine. If you want to talk that way, I will just go inside so you can do this all by yourself. Clearly you don't want anything to do with me so I will just leave." Ivy crossed her arms and held her nose high, trying to be confident and powerful even though she was clearly disappointed that she wouldn't be able to see what is inside the shed. Ivy then went inside and sat at the kitchen table, still pouting. "Man, I wish I could see what's in that shed today. Wait" that's when realization hit her. "This is my house! I can decide when I want to go! I live here. I can go anytime!" Ivy peeked outside the curtain to see if Madison went in or not. All Ivy could see was half of her body. Almost like it was split in half downwards. Ivy observed that her arms were crossed and she was tapping her finger on her left arm, like she was just waiting for Ivy to come out. She decided to go out and at least try to make her apologize.

The girls awkwardly walked toward each other with their heads to the ground. "I'm really sorry for raising my voice and being rude to you Ivy. I really am sorry." Madison spoke, she sounded pretty sincere and clearly owned up to what she did.

"Thank you." Ivy definitely forgives but never forgets. She will bring this up in the next argument they have-no matter the cost.

"Now," Madison took Ivy's hand and gripped tightly. "Let's go and open that shed. I'm sure that that stupid voice isn't even there anymore."

Two
Thin Ice

Both Ivy and Madison opened the door, tightly holding each other's hand. Then, very suddenly, a huge, dark hand, took both of the girls' waist. The girls screamed in horror as they got dragged into a hole. Ivy wondered why something this scary would come out of something this magical. The girls got dragged down a hole to what seemed to be underneath a light. The girls, falling and falling. A minute went by, still falling, then another, and another, and then another. Time seemed to be going slow. Almost as if they were falling in slow motion. The girls even had time to talk to each other. "WHERE ARE WE GOING" Ivy screamed.

"I HAVE NO CLUE," Madison replied, screaming. The girls could barely hear each other. Almost like the sound that was supposed to be in the hole got...heavy?

Both girls finally smashed into the ground.

Ivy rubbed her forehead and stared in amazement of what they had just fallen into. A teak brown forest and a crinkly floor. The trees would crack. But the sky was different. It was purple. The girls noticed a leaf-carpeted path and decided to follow it.

"What the heck? '' Madison said, scratching her head and looking around, slowly walking through the strange forest. "I have no clue what just happened." Right after Madison spoke, there was a rustle in the bushes. Leaves were falling off of trees. Someone was shaking it.

"Um...who are you exactly?" Ivy asked, peering behind the tree nervously.

"Me?" The strange creature pointed to himself and looked around, secretly hoping they were talking to somebody else. "Oh. I's is Fonic. Fonic Hornbrow." Fonic held out his hand, proposing to shake Madison's hand. Madison stared at his hand, debating. She stared and backed up, declining the hand shake. This creature was a dwarf. He was surprisingly nimble and well-dressed yet filthy and ragged. He was very tiny and had long horns coming out of his head. He also clearly had problems with his speech. "No. Way." Fonic was stunned for some odd reason.

"What is it?" Ivy asked.

"Yous guys is Ivy's and Madison!" Fonic

shouted . "All of the creatures have been talking abouts yous! Comes comes! We haves thing fors the girl in the...the brown jacket!" Fonic was clearly excited. Ivy pointed to herself, confused. "Yes yes yous! We've been talking about yous ever since yous moved ins! Yous has been chosen! Follow me!"

The girls look at each other and hesitate. They'd go of course. Who wouldn't want to follow a mysterious dwarf into what looked like an enchanted forest?

While walking, the girls examined the forest. All they could see were trees with beautiful leaves. They were unusual though. The leaves were every color you could imagine and more. Some of them even had a mix of two colors. For example, Ivy pointed out that one of the leaves had a mix of brown and almost an off gold. But the trunk was a very rich brown and was rough. You could see almost every piece of bark around the entire tree. But they were tall. Unusually tall. Taller than Ivy's twenty-foot high ceilings.

"These are magnificent. I wish I had trees like this." Madison stated while looking up and around, gazing at the trees.

"I don't. These are terrifyingly tall and- HAVE YOU SEEN THE LEAVES? THEY HAVE COLORS ON THEM. COLORS MAD-

ISON." Ivy shook Madison and stopped walking.

"Well what's you waiting for?" Fonic asked, annoyed. Madison noticed something about him though. It was his eyes. Something was wrong with them.

"Did you see that?" Madison whispered.

"No. What is it?" Ivy replied.

"His eyes were red." Ivy ignored Madison as she walked a bit faster than her.

About twenty-five minutes went by and they were all still walking. Fonic started walking ten times faster for some reason. Both girls walked faster as well to make sure they didn't lose Fonic and get lost. The problem with him walking fast was that Fonic was walking angrily. His arms and legs were tense and his arms were glued to his sides with the exception of his forearms. They were in an L shape, swinging back and forth as he walked. He had a curled lip and a clenched jaw. Madison noticed and didn't say anything.

After a while, Fonic started to look more furious at whatever it was. This is weird. Madison thought. "Well? Don't you think that Fonic is acting funny?" Madison said.

"Yes but you have to remember that we just got sucked into a random shed down a hole getting yanked down by a huge hand that grabbed us by the waist. What's a little grumpy dwarf?" Ivy said. Madison agreed and calmed down a bit.

All of them finally got to what seemed to be a castle. Fonic completely left them but the girls noticed something breathtaking. It was a huge tower with a stone wall guarding it. The girls noticed a platform and decided to step on it, each of them not saying a word. The floor rippled slightly as the stone opened and enfolded into a fire pit. The soil underneath their feet grew damp, and they felt the silvery veins in their skin extend and burrow like roots in the trunk of a tree, taking nourishment from the necessary sacrifice of a beautiful flower. "What the actual-" Ivy said. Both girls were confused but interested.

The ground would occasionally shake and grumble. Then, very suddenly, the girls' feet got cemented into the ground, soon forcing the rest of their bodies to become frozen. Not in fear, not in cold, but that they physically couldn't move. Madison and Ivy couldn't even talk.

A dark figure started approaching the broken stone, his eyes widening with madness. He was carrying what looked like a blade, long, sharp, and glistening with red damp blood. It was not possible to see his face. Just the shape of it. His entire body was silhouetted and he had a hat on. Almost like the ones you see in those secret spy movies.

Both girls were longing to escape but their bodies were frozen. They couldn't move. They couldn't shriek. They couldn't gasp. The shock had wrapped around their bodies, battling down their throats. The large figure just started getting closer and closer. Suddenly the girls didn't feel bored as they were when they were first stuck in the cement, not being able to move a thing.

"Hey girls, sorry I took so long. I was making my normal jelly sandwich with this incredibly huge knife." The figure said as he looked at his knife, front and back. "Oh my gosh I am so sorry about the whole 'not being able to move' and 'being stuck in cement' thing."

The girls looked at each other, confused and freaked out. With a swish of a finger, the dark figure un-did the spell. Madison immediately said something. "WHAT THE HECK MAN?" Madison began to talk fast. "I'm sure you were the one to drag us down in the first place and now you freeze us and then say you FORGOT about us? How? How did you forget about us? We were terrified of your 'bloody' knife and it was JELLY?! WHAT THE HECK MAN." Ivy was still frozen in fear and was staring at the figure.

The figure realized something strange about Ivy but chose to ignore it. He did notice though that she was the one that just moved in across from the shed.

"Come children, follow me." The dark figure told. The girls, very slowly, looked at each other with Ivy's look saying,

"Should we go in?" And Madison's saying,

"Well where else are we going to go?" The girls drew their attention back to the figure. He had his arms behind his back and was looking around, like he was trying to find something to do. Ivy and Madison walked towards him. Each girl holding the others' hand. The figure chuckled under his breath as he rubbed his hands together and his eyes grew wide. He started to turn around and then began walking. Madison was brave enough to start walking but Ivy was still shaking.

"Come on, hold my hand," Madison understood how scared she was and tried to comfort her as she held her hand out, proposing to hold Ivy's hand. Ivy quickly took her hand and they both started walking behind the strange, tall, dark looking figure. They were almost having to gallop to keep up with him. They were all 'galloping' on a long path. It was both light and deep, the spring sun interwoven with the shelter of the trees. The path before their feet felt as an invitation to their soles, that it wanted the girls to travel it and find out what lay upon it. It could have been there for thousands of years, perhaps it started in a place where time was truly forever, a place of eternal serenity. Each footfall was hard and rocky from below.

Ivy, Madison, and the figure were still walking after what seemed to be forever. Passing more and more interesting trees and colorful bushes. A couple waterfalls here and there. The girls even passed by a couple more dwarves. Some were woodworking inside trees and some were taking unicorn horns and running them through a machine. Although the girls hadn't seen any unicorns yet.

Ivy couldn't help but wonder what the dark figure's name was. He had to have one. What person doesn't have a name? If he even was a person.

All three of them finally got to what looked like a castle. The girls were speechless. The castle was bold on the blue beyond. It stood there as if conjured from the storybook of a child. It was perfect. Madison imagined unicorns in the courtyard, because if those towers could exist, why not? Every stone was even and square, as if those who built were set on perfection, as if they really loved what they made. There were walls made to protect a community, to echo with laughter and be the shelter they needed for the millennia to come.

"Are we going in there?" Ivy whispered,

"We must be." Madison whispered back.

"Come children." The dark man said.

The three of them walked inside and the first thing the girls noticed was the floor. It looked like it had been shaped over time by the soles of a family, of generations of living and loving right there. It had a rainbow of browns. Dark, light, in-between, anything you could think of. The walls were covered in gray and browns. But they were stone. The kind of stone that reflects sunlight onto the glossy floors. There were long and wide curtains draping over the huge windows. The windows were long and almost touched the ground and were very close to the ceiling. One of the windows was stained glass and let the imprint of the beautiful flower on the design of the window shine and fill the floor with the light of the sun. The stairs twirled upward toward the skylight, amid the rays that flowed upon them as bright water. The girls stood there, their mouths practically wide open as they stared in astonishment at what they had just walked into. They were so distracted that they didn't even notice that the man was already walking up the stairs.

"Come on. Let's go up the stairs with him."

Ivy said in her thick British accent while taking Madison's hand and quickly pulling her out of her gaze by dragging her up the stairs.

"Wow, look at this Madison." Ivy exclaimed while running up to an old record player. It was brown and leather. It had cobwebs blanketed all over it. Madison only took a glance over to the record player before shouting

"Ooo and this," Madison skipped over to an old closet with very old aprons and guns and even arrows. The man was standing with his hands interlaced in front of him. His face finally showed a bit. He had a large nose and small brown eyes. The space that the three of them had walked into was a big circle with the closet that Madison found interesting to the far right and the record player on a small table to the left of when you immediately walked up the stairs. A room was at the top of the circular room and looked like a hallway.

The girls decided to explore it because there was nothing in the circular room anyway. The girls made the right prediction of guessing it was a hallway because it was. Although the hallway didn't lead to anything. At least that's what they thought. The man walked slowly into the hallway with the girls.

"By the way, I didn't catch your name" Madison said, looking up at the tall, mysterious man who hadn't said a word since they were all outside.

"I don't want you to know my name nor are you allowed to know my name. Case closed. Stop talking and let me open this door." The man demanded.

Madison rolled her eyes. "Door? What door? There's no door in this short, narrow hallway." Ivy was confused. The man put his finger over his mouth as if he was telling Ivy to be quiet.

He had a key that he took out of his coat pocket that he stabbed into the wall. Yeah, you read that right. Stabbed. The girls' eyes both widened and they didn't say a word as they didn't want to be the next ones. They were confused though as to why that would 'unlock' the...wall in the tiny hallway. The mysterious man then started twisting the key in the broken plastered wall. For some reason he took the key out and put it in another spot in the wall. The girls were still speechless but mostly confused. Then, something strange happened. The wall started oozing out red runny goo. The girls didn't want to call it blood because they were already fooled by the jelly incident. The man twisted the key again but this time the red goo splattered all over the girls. They squinted their eyes hard and tensed their shoulders up.

The wall then opened up in the cramped

hallway. Ivy was amazed as she stared in astonishment at a huge palace-looking room, ignoring the goo all over her body. "Wow look at this Madison." Ivy muttered without taking eyes off of the candle-lit room. There was no response. "Madison? Madison, where are you?" Ivy was now worried as she quickly spun around and looked behind her. Neither Madison nor the man was there. There was no trace of them. No sound. Ivy couldn't even see the hallway they had originally walked into. Just a dark wall. She looked back in the room, there was only darkness. It was cold.

Yes, it was a dark room. But it was huge. All that was in the room was a table with a bunch of antiques on it. Globes, knives, china where, and a lot more that you can think of to be an antique.

There was something in the darkness of that room that was like a promise, like the world before dawn. It was a room as a canvas rather than a finished work of art, and to Ivy, it was all the more exciting. With each movement something new came to her hand, they looked like they were getting yanked off of that small table by an invisible person. The items started floating in midair and quickly made its way towards Ivy. A tiny fragment of furniture and antique ornaments took form, as if they were waiting for her to make them real.

Ivy didn't say a word. Just wide eyes and an open mouth, staring at every piece of antique she was unintentionally holding. "Keep these. You'll need them later." A female voice spoke. It was disembodied and echoey. Ivy quickly jolted her head up to the ceiling. Looking around for the voice.

Well what should I do now? Walk out like nothing happened? What about Madison? Where is she?

Ivy walked around the room a bit, holding the items and all. The room was huge. Ivy didn't know when it ended because it was so dark and she couldn't see anything beyond her nose. What she could tell while wandering around the room was that the room was round and the ceilings were very high. Suddenly, the lights turned on. The first thing Ivy noticed was the floors. They were a very light tan color. Like the ones you see on dance floors. "Where am I," Ivy whispered to herself.

Three

 A Guide to Giving up.

Meanwhile, Madison was banging on the wall in the small hallway. The man looked at his watch, annoyed. Madison was sobbing at the thought that she just got separated from her best friend.

Suddenly, Madison felt a big, warm, sweaty hand fix her hair behind her ear from behind. Madison knew it was the figure but stood frozen in fear. The hand then slowly began running his finger down the border of her ear, then to her cheek bones, slowly leading to her lips, his finger trickled up to the bridge of her nose and then suddenly wrapped his entire hand around her mouth, backing up and spinning around to make sure Madison didn't escape. She tried to scream. She tried to shriek. She tried to gasp. Madison noticed another figure approaching her. She tried to run but the hand holding her was too tight. The man kept getting closer and closer until finally, he yanked Madison's legs out from under her.

The two men began running–still holding Madison–into a dark, narrow, and cold hallway. Madison, crying and scared. The men brought her into a mysterious room. It was small and didn't have anything in it but a chair.

A chair with chains.

It was a white metal and the floor was completely concrete. The ceiling seemed to never end and the room had a soft breeze. Just enough to make the room extremely cold.

The men roughly placed Madison onto the chair and locked her up in the chains. The second the chains touched her skin, she immediately felt a burning hot sensation around her body. The heat began crawling up her spine and into her head.

She cringed as she rolled her head to make it stop.

Madison was finally able to scream. Her hands were tied up behind the cold chair and there was a thin piece of fabric blanketing around her mouth tightly. Yet the chains were hot and uncomfortable to even begin to worry about the fabric. As Madison glanced down at the chains slightly, she noticed something strange. Definitely unusual for chains. She realized that they began to grow extremely long spikes boarding around the outside. They were black and sharp. She knew that the spikes would eventually make their way into her skin. And she was right.

The spikes slowly trickled over the top of the chains and then inside of it. "Stop shaking, child." One of the men demanded.

She couldn't move one muscle.

The spikes became closer and closer to touching her skin. Finally, they did, enough to make indents all around her stomach. Madison got tingles and shivers all over her body. As the spikes pierced her skin, she felt something strange. Pain of course. But other than that she felt almost everything change.

Her vision was blurry and she felt the room spinning. The fabric on her face completely disappeared. So did the chains. Madison felt free and happy even. "Do you feel different?" One of the men asked.

"Yes. happy and free. But I feel–I feel–uhm–"

"Oh spit it out already!" He shouted. Madison stood up as she looked down at herself.

"What did you do to me?" She whispered as her voice cracked. Her eyes had a sight of terror and agony. Tears in her eyes as she realized that she was in pain. Deep pain. Not physically but mentally. First, she got torn away from her best friend, and now this.

"Well?" One of the men asked. "What do you feel?"

She took a deep breath but unfortunately didn't exhale.

The men smirked.

Madison was lying dead on the ground.

Maybe I'm in a waiting room of some sort. Ivy thought to herself, still trying to figure out what to do and why she was in that strange room. She had no idea what just happened to Madison but she did have a weird feeling about something going on. Ivy looked down at the items still in her hands and noticed a lightbulb. She felt a strange tingle to pick it up. As Ivy picked up the lightbulb, as she examined it, she saw a moving picture. It was Madison. Lying on the floor. Ivy knew it. She knew something was up with that strange man.

Ivy began to sob as she dropped all of her items and sat on the ground. She wept. A great tremor overtook her. She could hold the heartbreak no longer and she fell to the floor in a disheveled heap as her grief poured out. Ivy felt like she couldn't breathe but took deep breaths. Ivy has had panic attacks before that Madison has always helped her with.

Deep breathes Ivy. Deep breaths. Just stand

up and try not to think of it.

Ivy tried not to cry but she couldn't. It hurt too much. Madison was the missing puzzle piece to everything. Ivy knew she couldn't live without her. She tried her best to be happy. It's what Madison would have wanted. "What did I do wrong?" All Ivy could do at that moment was cry. She spoke to the lightbulb that still had Madison lying on the ground. "Madison, do you remember when we spent every holiday at my house?" Her voice cracked as she spoke. "We had so much fun together. We knew we were going to be friends forever." Ivy couldn't take it anymore. It hurt so much. Her heart was aching without her best friend.

For some reason Ivy was mad at Madison. She was mad that she didn't come to her for help. She was mad that she completely gave up. Ivy rewinded the video and she noticed that Madison didn't even try to fight back. Anger grew within Ivy. She didn't know why.

Stop being mad Madison. It's not her fault she passed.

But she couldn't help it. Yet she wasn't able to scope out why she was mad about Madison "not being able to fight back" She was vulnerable. She wasn't able to do anything about that. Suddenly, the wall she had originally entered opened up. Ivy looked back with tears in her eyes. She was glad that there was a way to get out now. She walked out and decided that she didn't want to be here anymore. So much has happened in the first hour she's been here. Including losing her best friend. Going down the stairs, Ivy became teary and ran to the doors.

As soon as she got out of that awful place, she wanted to go home. As she walked, she saw those colorful trees that Fonic had walked them by. She also felt someone brush her arm lightly. Weird shadow looking figures were zig-zagging between trees. The only reason they looked like shadows was because they were running so fast.

"Uhm...hello?" Ivy mumbled through her tears. Her voice got only one person's attention. It wasn't one of those short people that were gliding between trees. It was a boy. He seemed to be laughing before Ivy said something. He stopped what he was doing and peered up at Ivy. The boy had a sharp jawline and light brown fluffy hair. He seemed to be a little older than her but very tall.

"Oh hi!" He shouted from a couple trees in front of Ivy. His voice was dark but light at the same time. "Can I help you with something?"

"Oh I'm just curious about what's going on over here?" She chuckled through tears.

"Oh we are just having fun and getting some

energy out. It's really quite fun. I'm Leander. What's your name?"

"I'm Ivy," she sniffled. She was a little unsettled by the way Leander looked at her. She wasn't used to knowing for a fact that someone was listening.

"I love that name. Are you familiar with this neck of the woods?" He was very polite and thoughtful about Ivy and when she talked.

"No, I am not. I was actually heading out." Suddenly she felt a tingle cruise down her neck. She rubbed it as she said "I think I better get going."

"Going so soon? You just got here. Where did you come from to encounter me?" The boy raised his voice a bit as he invaded her personal space.

"The castle that's nearby. I really think I should go." Leander latched onto Ivy's wrist as she walked away.

"You can't get away that easily," He raised an eyebrow. "Let's walk back to the castle. How does that sound?"

"Actually, I would rather go home. Maybe you could walk me out?"

"Ha. You wish. Let's go." Leander's voice got higher through the sentence. He walked about ten feet in front of Ivy before he realized that she wasn't following. "Now." Leander said as he looked back.

Ivy gave in, hoping that he wasn't trying to trick her like the men did with Madison. Which she was still mad about. Madison didn't scream. Surly if she wanted Ivy to get her, she would've screamed. And Ivy would've heard her. Madison was everything she wanted in a best friend and more. Madison clearly didn't care enough to let Ivy help. That's what she was mad about. She didn't give Ivy a chance to help.

The two of them worked up some conversation while walking. "So let me guess. You moved into a new house and found a shed. The shed had a light and-" Leander proceeded to tell the entire story of how Ivy winded up there, not leaving out one detail.

"How'd you know?" Ivy was concerned. She never thought she would ever be stalked but for some reason the cute boy was one.

Why is it always the cute ones? Ivy thought.

"You probably think that I'm insane. I'm not, I swear. I just have a- uh- you know it doesn't matter. We are here anyway." Leander's phone rang. Ivy overheard him babble on about needing to be somewhere. She wandered off and gazed at the castle one more time. "I've got to go."

"Okay. See ya' around." Ivy smirked and walked into the huge castle doors again, sighing as she closed her eyes, stepping in one last time, praying, hoping that nothing bad or creepy would happen.

She strolled up the stairs and into the hallway. She spotted the key that the man unlocked the wall with on the ground. Ivy took the key and stabbed it into the wall.

The same thing that happened the first time, happened again. A dark room, and then the weird light, but something different happened this time.

Suddenly, someone spoke, snatching Ivy's attention.

"Hello Ivy." An embodied voice spoke.

"Um- uh hello,"

The voice grew louder as she spoke. "Now that you're here, I can speak. Shall I tell you about what-ifs and what-nows?"

"Who are you?" Ivy backed away from her as she asked, but she was near certain who she was–Madison, the essence of war and bloodshed. It couldn't be anyone else. She spoke again. "You've done something bad that you didn't even realize. The world will be mine. It was a lovely place. Chaos danced with me. The Lord himself dined at my table." That was not like Madison. Even dead it's not something she would've ever said. Madison squatted down in front of the fire. It was midday, but the room was overflowing and was dark with ash and smoke.

Is this some type of illusion? Ivy wasn't sure what to do.

"Madison? That's your name, right?"

"It's a name I use." She tilted her head at an odd angle and glanced at Ivy. "And you are that weird Ivy girl, the missing Water Queen, the one who was supposed to bring peace."

"What do you mean the 'missing Water Queen'?" Ivy felt that feeling again. A wave of sadness and confusion.

"You've been the Water Queen since you were in the womb. But you never came to acknowledge it. And, of course, I was never picked to be one." Madison spoke.

Ivy couldn't let those words get to her. But they did. She tried not to make it obvious. "Well then, I guess I am." Ivy could feel the heat of the fire as it grew wider still.

Madison's expression became hopeful: eyes wide, lips parted. "Sunlight and fire, much the same."

"No. I don't think so."

"You wouldn't be alone." Madison came close to Ivy and whispered.

"No." Ivy stood very still, sensing from Madison's predatory gaze that sudden movement might be unwise. "I should probably go."

"Don't you want me to answer your questions, Ivy? I know much."

"Is there a right response?" Ivy's words weren't wavering, but she felt certain that the ghost knew how intimidating she was. Hoping she wasn't making a mistake.

"Tell me what you will."

For some reason that was an awkward sentence for Ivy.

The fire became larger and larger. Ivy was furious at Madison now. She was only a ghost but was still as evil as a bad guy from reality.

Madison sauntered through the smoke-filled room; flames brushed against her like wild flowers in a field. "You see my what-if dreams...we draw nearer the war,"

War? What war?

"Little Water Queen. You made this war happen."

What? What did I do? I haven't done anything to hurt anyone.

The flames surged toward Madison, following in her wake. "You give me hope, so I give you a fair warning. You and I are in balance now. Follow your path, and I will owe you."

"Owe me what exactly?"

"Respect, fame...powers." Madison whispered while approaching closer and closer to the fire. The word powers got Ivy's attention. Ivy was never a greedy person. Feeling the need for powers confused her.

"Shall I snap him?"

"Who?"

"Leander. Shall I?"

"No."

"Shame." Madison sighed and looked at the sky. "It grows late, and I have others to see. My Lord will expect me to come soon."

And with that, the girl left her in the room reeling in disorder and panic.

She shall not 'snap him' under my watch. Ivy was hoping that 'snap him' didn't mean to kill him. She thought that it possibly meant physically breaking him in half but Ivy didn't want to think of that.

"What do I do now?" Ivy whispered to herself. She tapped her finger quickly on her thigh and bit her lip. She found the lightbulb that she had originally watched Madison in her pocket. She had a weird feeling to gaze into it again. It was Leander. He was walking into a weird cabin. But he was with someone. A girl. Ivy had only known the guy for twenty minutes but was jealous for some odd reason. The lightbulb began glitching and giving out. Soon, it was overflowing with darkness all around.

She was still locked in the room. She had

to be there for a reason. Ivy sat and pondered about the words Madison used to describe her. Stupid. Dumb. Those words quickly got to Ivy's head, no matter how hard she tried, she couldn't discard them. They were too powerful. Ivy then began believing the lie. I am stupid. I am dumb. Has she been thinking that our entire friendship? Ivy didn't doubt that she also thought she was too fat, or too boring, maybe even too rude. Sometimes Ivy thought that way about herself. Not as often as some people but she still thought it. She broke down in tears, hoping that Madison didn't actually feel that way about her. But Ivy now thought that way about herself.

People don't understand how words affect people.

She started to miss Madison. She was a ghost as she had just experienced but she was her best friend. It hurt to not have her in Ivy's life. Again, Ivy broke down in tears.

The wall opened up again and this time, Leander came out. He realized that she was crying and raced toward her. "Hey it's okay, I'm here now," He whispered, "don't forget that after the rain, sunshine returns, and crying is much the same, so let it out, let it out." He rubbed her back as he whispered.

"Sometimes it's sad, isn't it?"

"What is?" Ivy sniffled and spoke through tears.

"Sometimes the things we want to forget are also the things that once made us the happiest. Like Madison. It's okay to cry. It's okay to miss her. Don't think bad about yourself because of her." Ivy nodded as more tears raced down her cheeks. She wanted to tell him about how she felt about herself. So she did.

After proceeding to tell him, he thought for a moment.

Leander stood and looked down at Ivy. "I guess sometimes we stumble upon the thought of not being good enough. Not being good enough for our family, our friends, ourselves. The thought of failing crawls around our brain like a bug. Poking and picking at the fragile life we have left. Is that the situation you're in?"

Ivy was amazed at his incredible words. "Yes. Yes, that's why." She stood up slowly and wiped her tears.

"Well, don't give up so soon."

"Thank you, Leander."

He chuckled. "Yeah, I got it from somewhere in a poetry book or something."

Ivy slightly laughed through tears as she carefully wiped them away.

"We should probably get going now." Leander awkwardly walked toward the open wall and waited for Ivy. "Well come on now. We don't have all year."

Ivy was still hurt about what her best friend did to her. But more than anything she was angry. Ivy proceeded to walk toward Leander. She was quite awkward about it as well, given that Leander was watching her from across the room, still crying. This is embarrassing. She thought. "Where are we going exactly?"

"Oh, right, you're new to the village. Why don't I take you to meet the Lord?" Leander talked like he'd known Ivy for years. She thought that meeting the Lord was quite a big step up from what she'd been doing so far but she couldn't go home now. Not until she got her best friend back. "Come on now. Let's go." Leander smiled. His smile was pointy and from his eyes. Ivy gave in and followed him through the enchanting forest.

"What do you like to do for fun?" Ivy asked.

"Well, I like to play pranks. One time I set one of the dwarves' houses on fire." Leander chuckled at the thought. He jumped in the air and yelled, "Oh! Oh! And that one time I ate all of the food in the kitchen…we didn't have food for a week!" Ivy laughed so hard after he said that. She held her stomach as she laughed and even snorted a bit. Leander laughed at her laughs and that went on for about two minutes when someone caught Leander's eye. He stopped laughing.

"What's wrong Leander?" Ivy asked, concerned. She looked in his direction and noticed that he was staring at a girl. Ivy pouted but stayed quiet as he gazed at the girl.

"Wow." Leander giggled. "That girl is so unattractive." Ivy realized what was going on and laughed again.

The both of them laughed until their stomachs hurt and continued strolling down the small little pebbles. Ivy noticed that some were crystals. She had always been a big fan of rocks and crystals. Leander noticed how interested she was in the rocks when she stopped a couple times to look at all of the interesting rocks. Leander picked one up. It was an opal. He gave it to her and her face lit up when she held the cold stone in her hand. "Thank you," Ivy's voice was faint but was enough for Leander to hear her.

"You're welcome. Now, let's keep walking."

"Whoa. What's that?" Ivy was amazed. She was very interested in a huge log cabin she noticed, tucked behind a bunch of colorful trees.

"Oh, that's the keeper of memories. She's amazing. She can cure any illness and is immune from sickness. She is the wife of the legend, the one and only, keeper of love. He can fly, and even better, he has a breastplate of love- which is his armor. I guess he is an incredibly peaceful and honest person."

"That's amazing. What are their names?"

"Well, their birth names are Robert and Diana but they go by Fawn and Cosmo."

Four
Don't Die This Time

"Where is the girl?" The evil Lord asked.

"I don't know sir. I almost had her. She was so close to me I could've just snatched her. Ugh she's driving me insane." Madison thundered.

The evil lord snarled.

"It's your fault. You ordered me to get her but took her away from me!" She hissed.

The Lord sat up with a frustrated look. "How dare you blame me. You can't really blame me. You can only blame yourself. Do you hate me so much that you think I was the one who took her away? By goodness I would easily snap her neck in half if I had her." The lord huffed.

"I don't hate you," Madison said, crossing her arms, "I just strongly dislike you." She held her nose high, looking in any other direction that wasn't the lord.

"Don't ever say that to me again. I mean it."

"Fine," Madison replied, "I'll just leave."

She flipped her hair over her shoulder and began to march out of the castle. Her wings spread outwards and she began to take flight out of the castle and off of the cliff.

Madison was scanning out the entire forest, searching for Ivy. Oh if I could just get my hands on that stupid little- Madison's thoughts were interrupted by a strong gust of wind that forced her to shift indirectly. Up and over mountains she flew, around and around trees. Tall ones, colorful ones, and even the dead ones.

While gliding, Madison noticed a human. This was unusual for Madison because everyone in Eversect was some type of creature. "Hmmm," She whispered to herself, "sharp jawline, light brown hair, and not a dwarf, unicorn, or fairy." Madison made a satisfying face and shrugged, still gliding through trees. She sailed downwards toward the boy, trying to look at his face.

As she got closer and closer, sweat strolled down her cheeks and down her back. Her wings got heavier and heavier with every flap. She was tired. Upon Madison's arrival, she finally witnessed the face of this boy. "Leander?!" Madison screeched.

"Madison?!" Leander froze. They hadn't seen each other since he helped Madison out of the castle when she became evil.

Madison tumbled into the ground, dust going everywhere. As she cleaned herself off, she loudly asked, "Why aren't you with the lord?"

"I'm helping a girl. She saw a deer and went after it. A quite nice little creature if I do say."

"The girl or the deer?" Madison could barely hear her own voice because of her thoughts. What girl? I should be the only girl in his life. I guess we aren't dating but still.

Leander chuckled. "Both." He winked and rounded back to the trail. "Do you still hate me? Just because of my backstory?"

"Of course I hate you!" She struck his shin with her foot. "You told me you pretended to be dead for five years and then said to all of your friends and family 'sup?' Really Leander? Sup?"

"Calm down. It's not that big of a deal."

Madison ignored him and changed the topic. Crossing her arms, she said, "So who's the girl?" She propped an eyebrow.

"Oh her," He looked toward the meadow, "A girl. She's quite nice actually."

"What's her name?" Ivy was still crossing her arms. Both eyebrows were raised now.

"That doesn't matter. So how have you been?" Leander strolled down the trail, Madison didn't follow.

When Leander realized she didn't follow,

he stopped and gaped at her. Awkward silence infused the little rocks and pebbles that lay beyond the trail. "You comin'?"

"Mmm," Madison mumbled. She managed to slip in a little shrug and sigh and began walking. "How many questions do I have to ask? Where's the girl?" Madison urged.

"Oh, probably wandering. She's insanely curious." Leander replied. He caught on to the fact that Madison was somehow jealous. He showed little interest in her. But he knew. He knew that she was on the hunt for Ivy and couldn't let Madison get to her. Although he wanted to help both girls out, Ivy couldn't know that he knew Madison. Slowly, Leander could see Ivy's figure in the midst of all of the colorful leaves on the trees.

"What's wrong?" Madison asked. She gazed up at Leader. His sharp jawline, his long eyelashes, and his brown, fluffy hair. What a pretty boy. Madison thought. She snapped back into reality quickly and tugged lightly on his shirt after no response.

"Oh, umm, I think it's time I get going."

Madison considered that that was suspicious but knew she had to get going to the evil lord once again, to finish her next task or get screamed at again for not achieving this or that. Madison nodded at Leander, not saying a word, and flew off.

Her black, feathery wings took flight in the breezy air and left a slight wind on Leander's back.

"Leander!" Ivy screamed. "Look! Look! I found another cool rock!"

Leander chuckled and slowly walked toward the sprinting girl while scanning the ground. "So, what do you think about the cabins?"

She held the rocks close to her chest. "I think they are beautiful. I love the backstory between Robert and Diana...I mean Fawn and Cosmo," She put her hand in her pockets and stared at the ground. As she looked up, she asked, "Why do they hide their names?"

"Oh who knows. Probably some secret agency or something," Leander said sarcastically as he playfully shoved Ivy's shoulder.

She chuckled and began walking to the log cabins. They both awkwardly stumbled between trees. After a couple silent moments, Ivy was over it. This was way too awkward. "So, how long have you lived here?" Ivy questioned.

"Pretty much all of my life. I was forced into royal-" Leander cut himself off as he stared at Ivy. He cleared his throat, like he was uncomfortable.

Is there something in my hair? Is there something on my face? Neck? Eyes? Ivy's throat grew dry. "Is something the matter?"

"Nope. Nothing at all," He chuckled, "There is just some…uh…personal information I shouldn't share with you." He muttered.

Ivy shrugged and continued walking toward the cabins. Are we allowed to go in? Should I hold the door open for him? Or will he? Maybe I'll just open it myself. Yeah. That's what I'll do. She debated.

"Oh and just to let you know, they aren't home so we will only be able to look at them."

"Oh okay!" Ivy was glad she didn't have to overthink about how she was going to act or whether or not she should hold the door open for anyone. "Do you have any other friends?" She asked.

She can't know that I'm friends with Madison. I know they have an interesting past. What should I say? "Oh this dwarf named Fonic." He gestured toward the front of the forest while kicking a pile of wood out of their path.

"Wait back up, Fonic Hornbrow?"

"Yeah…do you know him?" Leander thought he made up that name.

"Oh boy do I know him. Long story. Anyway, let's keep walking along the trail, I can see the cabins from here. That's enough for me."

He chuckled as he glanced down awkwardly.

They worked up some conversation as Ivy began to wonder what happened to Madison after their little encounter.

Her thoughts were interrupted by a ringing and buzzing coming from Leander's pocket. "I gotta' take this," He mumbled. As he talked on the phone, his lips ran dry and his throat was like a cactus. He hung up and turned to Ivy. "Well, it looks like I have to go. Want me to take you back to the castle?" He said, trying to hide the fact that he was shaking with anxiety.

"No, I think I'm good." Ivy had always loved nature. The beauty, and the way the trees and mountains hold many secrets of so many people and creatures.

Leander hiked off and Ivy found her spot. The most beautiful spot she'd ever seen. Mountains that were gently covered with delicate fog and the few aspen trees burst with a blaze of bright yellow. Others were a bold green, prickly and tall. She sat at the edge of a cliff and gazed at the astonishing view.

Ivy's gaze was intruded by a strong gust of wind that blasted her hair into her own face. A loud flapping sound came from above. Ivy inspected the sky and covered her face from the blinding light of the sun.

"Well hello Ivy," A familiar voice spoke.

Ivy's shoulder tightened up to her jaw and her stomach was in knots. She knew exactly who it was. "Um...hello, Madison." Ivy said as she stood up and shook the gravel off of her hands. "What do you want from me now?"

"I think we should become friends again. I realize I messed up and I want to make it up to you. I feel terrible for what I've done. Please accept my apology."

Ivy was completely stunned. She didn't know what to do at that point. I love her dearly but she's done so many things wrong. I don't want to get hurt. Although, she didn't necessarily do anything bad to me. After several moments, she spoke. "I guess it wouldn't hurt."

"Great. Meet me here at 3:00 tomorrow." Madison ordered.

"Sure," Ivy said, nodding.

The next day approached and Leander came by to hang out with Ivy once again. Ivy had been stressing about what Madison said the previous day and decided to talk to Leander about it. "So apparently Madison wants to be my friend again."

"What?"

"Yeah. really weird, isn't it?"

"Why don't we go down to my place and talk about this. Who knows who could be watching and waiting y'know?" Leander said sardonically in a sarcastic manner.

When they got there, Ivy walked into a delicious smelling meal. Like herbs.

"Sorry, my place is kind of a mess. If you don't mind, will you help me make some supper?" He asked caringly as he scooped up some clothes from off of the floor.

"That sounds delightful. What can I help with?"

"Well, you can start by putting these herbs in a bowl and crushing them up," He replied.

She took the bowl and began crushing. Not taking an eye off of the herbs, she said, "So about Madison…"

"Yeah. Tell me more about that." He said sternly.

"She said she apologized for everything she's done. But I don't think she's done anything to me necessarily. I mean how bad could she be, really?" She picked up the bowl, still not taking eyes off of it, and spun around to the counter where the stove was.

He chuckled as he stirred pasta with one hand and sauce with the other. He dropped one of the wooden spoons in the pot and wiped his hands off with a towel with his free hand, shaking his head slowly. "I think you're being a bit too confident," he acknowledged.

"How? It's not like she's the worst person in the world." Ivy picked up some dirty dishes from the sink, turned on the faucet, put soap on the sponge, and began washing. "Who knows. Maybe she's turning over a new leaf."

"Ivy. I know a lot about her that you don't."

Ivy paused and looked behind her only to glare at Leander. When she looked back to the dishes, she began cleaning again but with raised eyebrows. "I've known her since the second grade. You've known her for three days. She tells me everything...Right?"

"I'm not so sure about that." He took the pot off of the stove and poured the pasta into a strainer in the sink right beside Ivy. "That girl could tear apart mountains with her own bare hands. She could burn down villages with a single glare. Heck, I wouldn't doubt she could take the throne of the Evil–" He cut himself off and poured the pasta into the pot, muscles tensed.

She turned around from the sink, leaned on the counter, and crossed her arms. "Evil what?"

"Oh, don't worry about it. I think I got a little carried away. Maybe she can't do all of those things, who knows," Leander kept thinking about how much Madison was forced to tell Leander. How much she changed and what she might do.

She rolled her eyes and headed for the door. "I better get going. I have to see Madison at three. Need help with anything else?"

"No, I think I'm fine, thank you."

She grabbed her coat from where it was dangling on the door knob and headed out without a "Goodbye."

When she got there, Madison was already waiting for her in a field of flowers, crossing her arms and tapping her finger on her upper arm.

What does she want from me? Why am I even here in the first place? Ivy's hands appeared to be shaking and her throat was dry and sore. Every lungful of hot air robbed more water from her body. Even when she swallowed as hard as she possibly could, her throat was still dry and icy cold.

Madison's facial expressions seemed far from relaxed. In fact, she seemed angry, confused even.

As Ivy approached, she uttered, "Why exactly am I here?"

"I need your help with something."

"With what exactly?" Ivy didn't think that that would come off as rude as it did.

"You know the Keepers? Fawn and Cosmo? Well, they need our help with something. They need us to keep the memories and love in a special place. You think you can help with that?"

Ivy hesitated as she relaxed her arms and fidgeted with her bracelets. "As long as nothing terrible happens, I don't think it'll hurt."

Five
Rude

The next day arrived and Madison was in the Evil Lord's castle once again.

"So?" The Lord longed for information from Madison.

"Sooo, I got Ivy to help with the plan. She doesn't know what she's in for."

The Lord evilly chuckled as he grasped onto a cold glass and elegantly sipped cold hard liquor. He gulped, licked his lips and said, "Good job. We've got her right where we want her."

Madison smirked.

The Lord took a deep breath and muttered, "Bring me the boy." He ran his finger along the rim of the cup as he waited.

"Yes sir."

The boy stumbled clumsily and gaped at the Lord.

"By gosh boy! You look like you've seen a

ghost! Am I that ugly?" He hollered.

"N-n-no sir." The boy stuttered.

The lord slowly sat back in his throne, not saying a word. He quickly looked at Madison, discarding his thought, "Leave us."

She nodded her head once and tensely walked out of the room.

"So. The girl–"

The boy cut his word off. "It's Ivy sir," His voice got quieter through the sentence, like he was regretting what he had said.

"Do you ever shut up?"

"Sorry sir."

"We speak elegant here, boy. I am sorry. Not just a silly old sorry."

"Noted, sir."

"We've got the girl. I need you to act like her friend. Lover even. Get close with her. And do not let her slip in between your tiny little fingers yet again!" The lord's voice boomed louder than storms raging over seas.

The boy flinched and slowly backed away, nodded slightly, and turned around bolting to Ivy.

Ivy was sitting on the mountains. Gazing at the elegant fog covering the mountains and all of the colorful trees. She took a couple deep breaths when Leander crept up behind her.

"BOO" His voice echoed throughout Eversect.

Ivy sprung up, startled. They both laughed a bit. "So?" Leander asked.

"So what?" Ivy questioned. Although she knew exactly what he was asking. Madison. She twiddled with her bracelets.

"What was going on with Madison?"

"Oh. Nothing really. I'm going to help her with something."

Leander's heart pumped fast. "With what?"

"Cosmo and Fawn–" She began collecting some rocks she found interesting– "They are on vacation and need help keeping the love and memories safe." She snatched a purple rock from the ground. Not even a glance at Leander.

He gulped. "Sounds fun. But wouldn't you rather stay at my place? We could watch a movie. Maybe invite some friends over?"

She stopped collecting rocks and slowly looked up at Leander. "Leander. This is my first time in Eversect. I want to be able to finally be able to help with things. I never got to do that back at home–" She studied the colorful pine needles on the trees– "I would always mess up–" She jotted down the interesting pine needles in her notebook– "And people would make me stop." She shut her notebook.

"Okay. Hopefully you don't get killed." He said jokingly and winked.

She snickered and shoved his shoulder with hers.

Leander flopped on the edge of the mountain, feet dangled off and hands clutched on the edge.

Ivy perched next to him. It was silent for several moments.

Leander gazed at Ivy but caught himself before she could look back at him. He quickly turned his gaze to the canyons below. "So did you take the offer?" He mumbled.

She rolled her head to look at Leander. "What offer?" Her voice cracked. A couple birds chirped in the distance, snatching Ivy's attention away from him.

He was quiet for a moment, then said, "Madison? Memories? Love? Ring a bell?"

She sighed. "Yes. Yes, I know."

"So? Did you say yes?"

She examined the ground, pondering why he wanted to know so bad. "Yes."

"Oh." He nodded his head and pursed his lips–like he was disappointed.

"Why is it such a big deal? I'm helping her."

"Madison isn't who you think she is, Ivy."

She stood up and gaped at the mountains, not looking at Leander. "She's turning over a new leaf. She's different now. What do you have against her anyway?" That came off ruder than I wanted.

He stood up next to her. "Ivy. She isn't innocent."

"You don't know that. You've barely met her."

He knew he couldn't tell Ivy so he sighed and stood there awkwardly. Leander glanced at the ground.

"So please."

He peeked at her blue high-top vans when she began talking.

"Let me do what I need or want to do. I don't need your opinion on whatever that is." Does he hate me now? I was so rude. Maybe I should apologize. Ugh. Too late for that.

He skimmed the ground and walked away with his head staring at the unique pebbles and moist soil blanketing them.

Ivy opened her mouth slightly to stop him from leaving but it was no use. She messed up big time. Ivy sat down again. It was comforting to gaze at the beautiful sight she got herself into. She put her headphones in. She liked to listen to dreamy music when she felt sad or numb. Which happened often. Ivy interlaced her fingers and put them in her lap between her legs, zoning out into space. It's happening again. I can't go through this again. She thought to herself. Ivy's life had felt like her life was a simulation ever since her best friend died and destroyed the entire world–almost.

After several moments she took to herself, she settled on the thought to go find Madison– why find Leander when it would be awkward anyway? She rose from the heavy rock she was sitting on and strolled down the path, taking her time to plan out where she would be going and what she would be saying.

Hey Madison…what's up…? She thought to herself. No no that's stupid. Ooh how about… um. Ugh this is stupid. She stopped walking and pondered for a moment. Maybe this is a bad idea. Ivy you're overthinking it. Where is she anyway? There seemed to be many voices in her head talking all at once. This is too over- whelming. Ivy took a second to look at the pine trees practically scraping her head. She looked up and took a pine needle off of the tree. As soon as she brushed them, they turned blue, like a watery type of blue. "What the…" She whispered to herself. As soon as she spoke, water came rushing down the tree for a split second. She gasped and bolted off.

Ivy ran as fast as she could, sprinting through trees and panting heavily. She smelt fresh rose- mary and thyme coming from somewhere–it was a familiar smell but she couldn't quite put her finger on where she'd smelt it before. It was on the tip of her tongue, just out of reach.

Ivy stopped to catch her breath but she found herself sitting on a large rock again, reflecting back to what that outstanding smell was. It was almost overwhelming how far she could smell it.

Ivy thought back to the morning and what she did. Leander's house! She thought. And off she went, sprinting between trees again just to find Leander. She had it in the back of her mind that she and Leander got into a little mishap but she didn't mind–all she needed was some advice on what she would say to Madison and if this is a bad idea.

Ivy saw a tiny cabin through the trees–Found it. Leander's house–she walked up silently to the doorstep secretly hoping he wouldn't an-swer. When she knocked, there was no answer. She waited for a couple seconds and again, no answer. Ivy creepily opened the door, it squeaked and cracked but no one was home. Maybe he overslept and didn't hear me knock. Or maybe he just didn't want to talk to me at the moment. Ivy didn't know what to do or think so she stepped in further. She never liked inviting herself over somewhere or to randomly walk into someone's house without them knowing (it was a quite awkward situation to be in)

There were no lights on, no music playing.

The teakettle sat on the burner. Two unwashed teacups were on the counter. It looked like Leander had gone out suddenly. "Leander?" She creeped into the kitchen–no one– she made her way to the bedroom–no one.

It was early morning, and the bed was already made. He'd left too quickly to wash his cups, but not too quickly to make the bed. Maybe he forgot to call. Or maybe he's running errands and didn't think I was coming. She knew it would be awkward if he came through the door while she was standing in his bedroom so she trotted out of the house quickly. Ivy slammed the door because she knew that the door gets sticky in the cold from the last time she visited.

Maybe Madison will know where he is. They seem to get along well. Ivy sauntered toward wherever Madison might be. I've never seen her house or where she lives so I have no clue where I should be walking. She pondered for a moment and thought of where Madison might've been. She's most likely at her house but I don't know where that is. Maybe a spot…a special spot…that we've both been. She thought. Ivy only knew that she was at Leander's house–other than that she was all turned around. Hmmm… "The castle!" She boomed as she darted towards the castle.

Wind was racing through her hair and her chest was pounding. Every breath she took got heavier and heavier. Birds scattered through Eversect as she ran, startled from the wind Ivy was creating. She didn't know where the castle was exactly but she knew she would find it–she always does. She slowed down a bit and thought back to when her grandpa taught her the directions and how to find places that she was unfamiliar with.

Look for the mountains.

She focused on places all around her but no mountains.

I guess I'll have to get used to no mountains. I do live in England now. Colorado is a big difference.

Enough time went by and Ivy finally got to the castle. She stood there inspecting the castle.

Here again. Bad, bad memories. She thought as she shook her head and slowly strolled, not taking an eye off of her feet. Ivy didn't think about where she should go or what she should say to who. Ivy, practically shaking with fear and a dry throat, knocked on the door loudly.

Maybe I knocked too hard. It is a big castle though. Maybe people didn't hear the knock.

She waited for a couple seconds, standing there awkwardly. She heard footsteps and a familiar voice–definitely not Madison's. Someone opened the door and Ivy's eyes grew wide as she slowly walked backward. Who was standing at the door you ask? The one and only Leander.

"Madison? You aren't supposed to be–I mean, what are you doing here?"

"Well you can't expect me to sleep outside now do you? I went looking for you at your cabin but no one was home so I came here to look for Madison." She said, inviting herself inside. She glanced around a bit.

Those red carpets, and the stairs leading to the circular room with the hidden door. Bad memories.

Leander couldn't think of what to say. "Okay um… come on in. Madison should be in the back."

Ivy began walking through the hall before Leander positioned his hand right in front of Ivy's face, stopping her from walking any further. "Actually, I'll get her for you. Just–stay here please."

She stood at the doorway awkwardly because she didn't know what else to do.

Something shiny caught her eye.

I'll just go into this room. That's it. No further.

As she ambled toward the room, the light

got brighter and brighter.

What could this possibly be? She thought as she plucked it off of the wooden table it was lying on.

As she collected it, she felt the tips of her fingers start to burn.

Ouch. It's really, really hot.

And it only got hotter from there. As she placed both hands on it delicately, there was no choice but to drop it.

"Ouch!" Ivy hollered. Her voice echoed through the thick castle walls.

Ivy examined the castle, just to make sure no one heard her scream.

She carefully picked up the shiny thing from the ground. It was still hot but it wasn't as shiny.

Hmm. This is weird. It's just a lightbulb.

But it wasn't just any old lightbulb. It was special. Like she'd seen it before. Like she'd touched it before. And like something odd had happened with this lightbulb before. Ivy tried hard to recall what had happened before with this odd trinket.

I've definitely had it in the castle before.

"That's it!" She whispered. "When I was in the castle last, this very lightbulb showed me what Madison was doing and when! Maybe I'll use it now…?" She questioned herself. She couldn't recall how it worked. She thought maybe rubbing it like a lamp would do some sort of magic–somehow. She began stroking it gently and saw Madison carrying something, it looked like sparkly dust, and somehow Madison was carrying it with her own two hands.

Ivy squinted her eyes tightly, confused. Then, she saw Leander, rushing in and hollering at Madison. Ivy's eyes became wide now as she set the lightbulb on the table carefully and backed up slowly. The images on the lightbulb began to fade as Ivy's breath grew heavier.

Leander entered the room, out of breath. "Sorry it took a bit, I was trying to get Madison out of work but-"

"You work with her?!" Ivy was furious.

"Um– well it's uh…complicated…I guess." Leander stuttered.

She began passing.

"What's the big deal?"

"You know she's evil right? You work with a crazy person!" Ivy screeched with rage and got close to Leander's face–very close.

"Whoa Whoa Whoa! She can't be as crazy as you are right now!" Leander tried to lighten the mood with sarcasm but knew he failed when he saw her furious face.

Eyebrows were lowered and close together, eyelids squinted in rage, lips were tightened, her jaw was tensed and pulled forward, and her fists were closed tightly as she breathed heavily.

"Okay, Ivy. I promise I don't do anything evil and neither does she. She's better now."

"Do you guys work for someone evil?" She asked.

He hesitated. "No…"

"Good. Let's go." She lightened up.

He was confused on what just happened and why she switched moods so quickly. Girls. He thought.

Ivy walked confidently out of the doors to the castle.

She stopped and paused for a moment.

Leander, practically, crashing into her, said, "What? Why'd we stop?" A couple moments went by and she was just standing there foolishly. "Well? Don't leave me hanging!" He turned to Ivy and cleared his throat. She looked like she was calculating something.

Very suddenly, Ivy clenched onto Leander's shoulders and shook him slightly. "Did Ivy ever get a hold of the memories? Or love?"

Leander was a bit shocked from the sudden movement Ivy had made but answered somewhat quickly. "I'm not sure. Why do you ask?"

She began to walk briskly out the door as Leander followed. "Well, I saw her through the lightbulb and a pink, sparkly dust caught my eye. I'm thinking now that that might be the–"

"Whoa Whoa Whoa. Back up," He interrupted, "What lightbulb? What does it do?"

She groaned. "Long story short, I found this lightbulb when I was in the castle last and it showed me what Madison was doing…kind of like Beauty and the Beast with that mirror!"

"Beauty and the Beast?"

"Have you never seen it?"

"Um, no?"

"You must not have television." Ivy took a deep sigh.

Together, they strolled out of the castle. Ivy was still a bit rattled by the fact that Madison might have the memories or love.

Six

333 / The Lesser-Known Brother of 666

The lord had just entered the room when Madison put the memories in a big jar. She titled it with elegant letters reading:

Memories

"How are we doing over here Madison?" The Lord peered over Madison's shoulder.

"Pleasant sir. I just got done with the memories. We can carry on with the plan."

"Which is?"

"To steal the love and memories from Fawn and Cosmo and take over Eversect. Right?"

"That's right." the Lord nodded.

Madison made an amusing face and began stirring some potion.

"I will be back to check on you. I've got the girl." The Lord winked.

As he marched out, he rehearsed how to sound convincing with the girl. He would make eye contact.

He would sound calm yet stern.

And he would make sure absolutely no one blew his cover.

He approached Ivy.

And as she circled towards the Lord, her eyes grew wide. "Leander," She mumbled. Leander was still walking even though Ivy was tugging on his shirt. "Leander!" She growled. Ivy leaned towards Leander's ear and whispered, "that's the guy who–"

"Before you speak any further," the Lord held his hand out, "I was wondering if you were to know Madison by chance?" He made sure to keep eye contact, although he thought he might've been a bit intimidating.

"Yes, yes I do know of her. Why do you ask?"

"I happened to just be talking with her. You are helping keep the memories and love safe, right?"

Ivy paused as she glanced at Leander. He still had a foolish look on his face. "Yes, I thought so."

"Okay then, Ivy, I need you to go collect the love for me then. Madison has got the memories taken care of."

"And how do I–"

"You will travel up and down hills to Fawn and Cosmo's house. Do you understand me girl?"

"Yes sir."

"Then run along, we've got no time to waste." He had a devilish smirk on his face.

Ivy and Leander began walking toward the log cabin. "Am I the only one that thought that that was a bit weird?" Ivy said, finally breaking the awkward silence.

Leander didn't know what to say. He would normally make a joke out of it but for some reason he felt very uncomfortable.

She waved her hand in front of his face, trying to get his attention. "Hello? Earth to Leander," she said, annoyed.

"Oh, sorry. Lost in thought I guess."

"So? Was it weird to you?"

"I guess it was."

Then there was silence again. Crunching of the dirt and leaves oddly broke the awkwardness, at least for Ivy. She could smell fresh herbs coming from Leander's garden.

We must be close to his house.

She glanced over at him, thinking that it was weird he hasn't made any dumb jokes lately. "Hey are you okay?" She asked.

"Me? Oh, yeah, I'm good. Just thinking."

She took a deep sigh and stared at the ground, not knowing what to say after that.

"Hey we're here!" He hollered.

She chuckled a little. "So do we just go inside?"

"I think so. Maybe all of the love in the entire forest is just lying on their counter top."

There's my Leander. She giggled, "I mean who knows!"

They laughed.

Together, they walked up the long stairs leading to the cabin.

Leander quickly opened the door for Ivy.

She looked at him and smiled, walking in. She immediately smelt a faint earthy scent that all cabins seemed to have. "So where do you think we should look for it?"

"The Lord told me that–"

"Whoa Whoa Whoa. The Lord? The Lord told you what? How did you get a hold of him?" She felt herself get angry.

Leander knew he messed up but knew he had to tell Ivy at some point. "Look, Ivy, I should've told you this a long, long time ago, but I–"

She shoved him away forcefully. "You work for him?! How could you do this to me?" Her voice cracked.

"Ivy, I am so sorry."

"You work for the evil Lord," she began to sob, "He killed my best friend Leander."

"I know, I know. I worked with him before all of that even happened, Ivy." He anxiously walked over to the stone countertops as she followed furiously.

"Were you in on the plan?" She asked.

"On killing your best friend? Of course not. I mean…I guess I was involved in…some way. Not like I planned it or anything. I was forced."

She grew silent. "Whatever. Let's get the love and get out of here."

Leander scrambled through some boxes while Ivy observed some shelves over the bookcase. "Can I ask you a question, Leander?" She questioned.

"Didn't you just ask me one?" He chuckled, trying to lighten the mood.

She gave him an unamusing look and said, "Leander. This is not the time," He lost his smile and looked through the boxes again, "were you using me to get information for the Lord? And, I guess, Madison?"

"I wouldn't do that to you. I care about you Ivy. I would never in my entire life try to hurt you."

He sounds genuine but I still don't know if I should forgive him. Not for a while at least.

She felt tears filling up in her eyes. Her vision got blurry and a lump formed in her throat. A great sob escaped her, and she covered her face with shaking hands. She then would wipe her cheek every few seconds. Her heart was broken. She never thought that Leander would betray her like this. "I thought we were good friends. I really did."

"We are still good friends. Just because I work for him doesn't mean I'm any less a friend to you."

She found the jar of love sitting on the fireplace. Wiping her tears with her sleeve, she said, "Whatever. Let's just get out of here."

They got outside of the cabins and Leander began to get mad that Ivy didn't believe him. "Honestly Ivy, it's a shame that you're like this. All you do is jump to conclusions." He ran off to his cottage, leaving Ivy behind.

She found the cliff she used to sit at and decided it was a good time to relax and look at the view, to get away and forget everything.

She sat for a long time. A rustle in the pine trees broke the silence that Ivy was enjoying. She peered behind her, not really caring what was in the trees anyway. She figured it was Leander trying to scare her again. "Go away."

"Ivy," She bolted up from the ledge, "Did he leave you?"

"Madison!" Ivy ran up to hug her.

She laughed and sat on the cliff with Ivy. Ivy told her the story about what happened with

Leander.

"That sounds awful," she said softly, giving Ivy an awkward side hug. "I am so sorry."

She smiled and pulled out the jar of love from her pocket. Madison gave a smirk and snatched it from Ivy's hands.

"I should get back to the castle now," Madison said excitedly.

All Ivy did was smile and look at the ground. It's all she could do without crying at this point.

The Lord suddenly appeared behind her. She jumped and stood up facing him.

"So, I hear from Madison that you've betrayed your friends," he said in an oddly comforting voice.

"Leander says it's a shame that I'm like this."

"Like what? A maniac?"

"What? How am I a maniac? I understand that I can cause a panic but I was just excited to be useful to you." She turned sad throughout the sentence.

The Lord discarded her thought, "You're lucky to be so gifted for a Water Queen."

"That's got nothing to do with it–"

"Don't fret."

"I am not afraid of you," She found her voice again.

He gave her an engaging look, "For

now."

Ivy, now frightened, stood up and marched away, arms crossed and all.

She took a moment to process it but eventually realized that the Lord was using her, which led Leander to use her too. Ivy was absolutely convinced that Leander was using her.

Thoughts aren't always true.

She began to walk slowly with her hands in her hoodie pockets, looking at the ground. She put her earphones in like she always does when she's sad or confused. Ivy has always needed to take a moment to think over what had happened before she could talk to anyone. So, she took a moment to do so.

She came across the castle and took a moment to gaze at it. She started to smell rain and pine trees, like she always does when she comes near the castle. Ivy took a big step and knocked on the big wooden doors, one hand still in her pocket. As she waited for someone to come to the door, she turned off her music.

Madison opened the door. "Ivy! I am so happy to see you! I have big news to tell you."

"Okay okay, at least get me inside first!" She smiled and trampled inside.

Madison sat Ivy down on the red leather couches in front of the burning fireplace. "What did you need to tell me?" Ivy said, holding her hot chocolate.

"I recently found out that," Madison took a glance at Ivy, "Ah maybe I shouldn't tell you."

She sat closer to Madison. "Pleeeeeease?"

She had no expression at all on her face. Just a blank stare at her feet scraping the carpet underneath the couch. She sighed.

Ivy started to get a bit suspicious and wondered what was taking so long. This can't be good. She thought.

"I recently found out that," She took a deep breath, "Your parents have contacted you. They are really worried and apparently sent out search parties."

Ivy felt her stomach drop. Her heart pounded louder and louder as she felt the need to cry. Are they mad at me? I don't want them to be worried. I need to find a way home. "So how can I fix this?" Her voice stayed even throughout the sentence, "How do I get home? How do we get home, Madison?"

"I can hear the panic in your voice. It's okay. No need to worry. We have got this all figured out."

Ivy spaced out and swallowed hard. "How did you even find all of this out? I deserve to know."

"A dwarf came in a while ago and told us. And trust me, I have no idea how he found out."

"So how do I find my way back home?"

Before Madison could answer, they heard a voice coming from the other room. "Madison! Madison! Come over here and work on these potions!" The Lord boomed.

Madison huffed, "I have to go. I'll come back to you on that, okay?" She ran off and didn't look back.

Ivy was frustrated that she didn't tell her but walked outside the castle doors and plugged in her music again. It was starting to rain and thunder. Ivy's favorite type of weather. Something about it was comforting. Probably the smell or the loud sounds the thunder makes, maybe even the flashing lights the lighting makes over the streams and rivers.

It began to pour and pour some more. She put her hood up and ran over to Leander's house. She figured it was time to figure out what had happened between them.

When she finally got there, she was hesitant to knock on the door. Ivy, it will be fine, he's not a complete stranger. She told herself.

He opened the door and sighed, "Cold out there, little girl?"

Well, he seems quite happy. Maybe this won't be so bad. She laughed and invited herself inside. "I'm sorry for what happened back there. I let my thoughts get the best of me and jumped to conclusions. I shouldn't have been so mean about it. I hope we are still good friends."

He pulled out a chair and a blanket for Ivy. "Thank you. I am sorry as well. I shouldn't have run off and been immature about it."

"Thank you, Leander."

He nodded. "Coffee?"

"Sure."

He proceeded to get a coffee mug out of the cupboard. "You and Madison seem to be better friends."

"Yeah I guess so," She took the coffee out of his hands and took a tiny sip, "Speaking of, she just talked to me and informed me that my parents have been looking for me. They think I've run away."

He sat down in the chair next to her with his drink. "That sounds stressful. How can I help?" He held her hand gently.

Her heart rate increased as she stared at her hand. She swallowed before she said, "I think you being here is enough for me."

He smiled slightly. "I wouldn't worry about why they think you left."

Her knees were tucked away in her chest as she hugged them with one arm and held his hand with the other. "They say I ran away. Did I run away?"

Silence followed a deep breath from him,

"Do you think you did?" He came closer to Ivy to look at her.

"I don't know, if they think I betrayed them, I want them to know that I'm coming home."

He didn't know what to say to that.

"I want to go home, Leander."

He waited to answer, "And where is home?"

"From here, a long, long way. I think Madison is the only one who knows where it is and how to get back." She took another sip of coffee, holding the mug with her sleeves.

"Let's go find her then," he said in a tone that was calming to Ivy.

She sat up and let go of his hand. "It's pouring out there." She said as she walked toward the small window and peeked outside at the garden Leander was growing.

He followed. They both looked outside together. Ivy loved watching rain. She and her parents used to do it when she was a child.

Leander gave her a side hug. She was hesitant but eventually rested her head on his shoulder.

Moments passed and he finally asked, "Would you care to stay tonight? I can't have you sleeping outside again."

"That would be lovely." She usually denied offers like this, but really did need a place to stay. She figured it would be nice to have some company.

"Great! We can make some popcorn and watch movies, maybe even play some board games too!"

She laughed and nodded but her thoughts were going crazy. He seems to be really excited. He doesn't like me…right? She glanced at the white numbers on the microwave clock. 6:32, She thought, I wonder how late he normally stays up.

"I'll start making some dinner. Anything specific you would like?" He asked as he brought a pot out of the cupboard and placed it on the stove.

"I'm open to anything." She announced as she wrapped a blanket around her and put her head on the counter, facing him.

He smiled and tilted his head at her, like he was in awe. "I'll make some spaghetti."

She nodded and closed her eyes, not exactly asleep, just resting.

He took a look at her and smiled. I don't blame her, she has to be tired after all of this stress. He thought.

She opened her eyes again and observed him cook. Something about it was satisfying.

"Suppers' ready." He whispered.

All she could do was nod, she was so tired. Ivy sat straight up against the chair, still wrapped in the blue fuzzy blanket Leander gave her.

He set a bowl of spaghetti and garlic bread in front of her.

"Thank you," she murmured.

"My pleasure, Ivy." He answered as he pulled out a chair and plopped down with his bowl. "Anything to drink?"

"Nope."

"Great. I wasn't gonna get you anything anyway," He joked.

She snickered as she lifted her fork and began eating.

When they were finished with dinner, they sat on the couch and debated what to watch. "I thought you didn't have a television?" She almost-asked.

"I do, I just don't know what beast and the boot is." He laughed.

She busted out laughing, "Beauty and the Beast?!" She snorted.

He laughed with her, "Oh whoops!"

She calmed down and asked, "Why don't we watch that then? It's a really good movie."

"Sure. But is it going to be one of those mushy romance movies? I hate those."

She giggled, "I suppose it is a little bit."

He made a jokingly disgusted face and glanced down at her.

They began watching and munching on their popcorn gradually.

The next day arrived. They had already eaten breakfast and gotten ready when she heard a knock at the door, she ran to open it. When she did, Ivy was quite surprised. It was Madison.

Ivy wasn't the only one surprised, though, Madison went ballistic. "What do you think you're doing here?"

"Well, it was raining so I thought I should–"

"I don't want to hear it. Where is he?" Madison didn't wait for Ivy to respond, all she did was shout, "Leander! Leander!"

"He's in the back."

"Doing what?" Madison was furious for some reason

She is so jealous. Ivy kind of liked it–the thought of her being jealous–she didn't know why. "Chill. He is in the shower. What do you need him for anyway?" She raised her eyebrows.

"I need him for–"

And with that, Ivy slammed the door right in her face.

Leander slowly walked out of the bathroom, hair wet, and wiping a towel over his face to dry it. "Who was that?"

She gulped. "It was Madison. I guess she

needed you…I guess."

"You seem nervous."

"Why would I be nervous? Anyway, you should get going to the castle. It must be a big deal if she has to come all the way to your house to get you. Wouldn't you just go to work anyway? And see her there?"

He laughed under his breath, "Yes I would. Are you done?"

She nodded and gulped again.

"Then I am going to get dressed and ready." "Okay."

When he was done, he said goodbye to Ivy, "I will be wandering around the forest a little bit around twelve if you would care to join me." He said as he hugged her.

"That sounds great." She said, hugging him back.

"Meet you at the rock," He snatched his leather coat off of the hat rack and jolted out the door, "Don't forget to bring a sweatshirt. It's chilly out here."

"I will be sure to do that." I wonder if he thought that sentence was too awkward. It was awkward to say. I should've said "Okay great."

After a couple minutes she let that thought go and thought that wandering Eversect was a wonderful idea. She grabbed her sweatshirt as Leander recommended. It was her favorite one.

The blue one that her grandma crocheted for her. It was small but it was special.

She toddled out of the door and strolled to the rock. It seemed a lot closer to his house then she remembered, Ivy relaxed on the edge as she had always done. She put her earbuds in and gazed at the view.

She eventually got lost in thought, smelling the scent of rain every time she inhaled. She felt the moist rock beneath her and the subtle breeze flowing through her hair.

She was relieved that there were finally no interruptions. Ivy stood up and placed her hands in her pocket, deciding not to talk too much to herself, she had always worked up conversations with herself that got annoying over time.

Ivy strolled down a trail she found and recognized it from when Leander took her by Fawn and Cosmo's cabins. She felt a gloomy drizzle start up again. She adored it. Ivy didn't know where she was going or where she would end up, as long as she didn't get lost, she didn't care.

Maybe I'll go visit Madison and Leander. Couldn't hurt.

When she arrived at the castle, she knocked on the big wooden doors as usual and waited for an answer.

To her surprise, a dwarf answered. "Who's

you comin' in for? Why's you here?"

"I am looking for my friend. Would your name perhaps be…Fonic? Fonic Hornbrow?"

He stared at her. "Yes. Ivy is it? Come on in." Fonic led her to what seemed to be the living area. "Whos you lookin' for?"

"Um, Madison, and if possible, Leander."

"Leander?"

"Yes. Leander. Is he not available?"

All he did was gawk at her. He tucked his clipboard underneath his arm and tapped his lip with his pen. "I do not recall any Leander persons."

"What? I thought he worked here? With the Lord."

"I'll go gets Madison fors yous."

Weird. He has to work here. Unless he knows something I don't. I know Madison doesn't work here though. She just likes to hang around, I guess.

Madison came out holding that same weird dust Ivy saw in the lightbulb. "What's that?" She asked.

Madison quickly put it behind her back. "Nothing. Why are you here? Need Leander?"

"Actually, I was hoping for either one of you."

"Why?'

"No reason," She slowed her words, "Just

needed some company I guess."

Madison stared at her awkwardly. "Did you get the company you needed?"

Obviously, Ivy was hoping for a lot more time but thought it was weird to ask again. So she nodded her head and flopped on the couch as Madison walked off, still caring that weird pink dust.

Why wouldn't Fonic know of Leander? He works here after all. I'll have to talk to Leander about it when I see him soon. She thought. She glanced at her watch. 11:30.

Eventually, she fell asleep until about 12:15. When she woke up, she sprinted out of the doors and ran to the rock to meet up with Leander. She was eager to ask him about why Fonic didn't know of him.

She arrived and found Leander sitting on the rock, gazing at the trees and the mountains. "Hey," she said, out of breath.

"Hey what's up?"

"Nothing. I was just at the castle." She commented.

He looked at her confusingly. "Why's that?"

"I was hoping for some company while I was waiting for time to pass."

He nodded, not saying a word.

"Something wrong?" She asked.

"Nah. Did you ask for me?" He seemed worried about the answer to that question.

"Actually, I did. I wanted to ask you about that. Fonic said he doesn't know of any Leander that worked there." She lowered her eyebrows a bit. "Anything you want to tell me?"

Leander took a deep breath. "Ivy," He cupped her right hand in both of his, "I should have told you this a long time ago." He hesitated. "But um, it's getting a bit late, catch you later okay? My place, seven 'o'clock."

Before she could utter a word, he had already left. She felt devastated because all she wanted was to know what was going on. He didn't seem to want her to know. Ivy had always been a people pleaser. She had always wanted to be the person that everyone trusts. Not being that to one of her best friends felt like she wasn't good enough. It sounds crazy but it's true.

Seven
So?

The afternoon flew by and Leander returned to his little cottage. He saw Ivy sitting on the rock but didn't bother to say anything. He didn't want her to ask that awkward question again. When he stopped inside and flopped all of his supplies on the countertop, he immediately called Madison.

"Hey, I didn't tell you this earlier but Ivy is on to me." He sort-of-whispered.

"And how did you manage to let that happen?" She didn't sound that stern nor mad but he still knew she was frustrated somehow.

"I have no idea," He opened the fridge, "Apparently she talked to Fonic and he didn't know of me." He said as he closed the fridge.

"And she asked you about it?"

"Mmm." He peered out of the front window, pulling the curtains away, and focusing on Ivy. "She's outside my house right now. I don't want to go out there because I want to avoid the question at all costs."

"Got it."

There was a still moment of silence as he stared at her once again.

"Well, I gotta go." she seemed in a rush to leave.

"Okay talk to you later I guess." He hung up.

Leander paced around the couch, needing an answer from someone on what to do. I need to figure this out. I don't need help for everything. He thought. It's what his dad said to him anyway.

He strutted outside and sat next to Ivy. He didn't know what he was going to say, but he felt like it was going to go well. "Hey." He mumbled.

She didn't say anything.

"What's up?"

No answer.

"Doing okay? I'm ready to talk about… y'know…earlier."

She nodded.

He needed to get it over with but he also needed to sound confident. "I'm immortal." He said, squinting his eyes.

"What? What does that mean?" Ivy looked at him weirdly.

He sighed and took her hand again. "In this forest, immortal means that I'm not actually here. You live forever but no one can see you unless you're either part of the court, or," He took a second and paused, like realization was just hitting him, "or if you're royalty."

They looked at each other. "Are you royalty?" He asked.

She took a moment to think, "Madison has told me that I'm a 'water princess' but I don't believe her. I guess now I should, unless I'm a part of the court." She laughed.

He didn't laugh back. "You're a princess?"

"I guess. But honestly, I don't even know what that means or what I'm supposed to do. And she did say water queen."

"Ivy. You're a water queen?"

"Didn't we just establish this? Like, two seconds ago?" She said, standing up.

"Sorry, sorry. Um, we need to get you to the evil lord." He snatched her wrist and dragged her to the castle.

"Why?" She practically yelled.

"You'll see," He shouted.

When they got there, they scurried up to a big dining room where the lord was. Leander greeted him with "Hello."

The lord was sitting at a very long dining table and glanced up from his food. It seemed to be smoked salmon. "Dare interrupt me boy?" He saw Ivy and immediately seemed calmer. "I see you've got the girl."

Ivy looked at Leander, like the lord was proving her point of Leander using her for information.

"Yes, yes I have." He stuttered, like he was nervous for some reason.

"What am I doing here and why do you want me?" she spoke.

He quickly turned his head to look at her. "Why, you are the Water Queen my dear."

"Why is everyone making such a big deal out of that?"

Leander tensed.

"My God, where are your manners woman? Do you need to be sent to the dungeon?"

She gulped, "no, sir."

He nodded once. "As I was saying, you are the Water Queen. Meaning you will rule the forest."

Her heartbeat ran fast.

Leander could tell on her face that she was scared to say anything because of what had happened moments before. He wanted to comfort her but couldn't. He wouldn't want to risk looking weak.

"So, what does that mean for me?" She asked.

"Well, Ivy," He breathed deeply, "you would simply be all-knowing and all-seeing. You would know everything that happens here in Eversect. That is, if you accept it."

She exchanged a glance with Leander before answering. "Do I have any time to think about it?"

The lord thought for a moment. He took a bite of his food, chewed, swallowed, and finally said, "fine. Two days."

"Yes, sir."

"Now leave me."

Leander took her arm and led her outside. "So that happened," He commented.

"Yeah," She sighed. "So, what should I do?"

"I'm not the queen, your majesty." He said jokingly with a bow.

She laughed.

"Do you want to take some time? You can come back to my place and we can figure it out together. I mean, unless you want to be alone, I won't force you to be with me or anything." That did not go as planned. I sounded too nervous.

She giggled. "It's okay," he smiled at her, "we will just think about it together."

They began walking as one, their arms occasionally brushed up against one another. He would get butterflies with every accidental touch. Though he would never admit it.

As he peeked over at her, he caught her glaring at the ground. She looked nervous, or maybe really concentrated on the intriguing rocks.

It was silent again. But he was okay with it. He felt comfortable. Like it wasn't as awkward or tense.

"What are you going to do?" He asked.

"I don't know. I want to go home but I love the forest so much."

Leander didn't know what to say that would help. All he could think of were jokes to lighten the mood. "Yeah."

She shrugged and continued to look at the ground.

Maybe I wasn't confident enough.

Ivy followed him inside. They sat on the two barstools that stood in front of the wooden countertops. "So?" He subtly questioned–assuming she knew what he was talking about.

She took a deep sigh–enough to raise and lower her shoulders with a single breath. "I don't know. How would I get home? Y'know– if I chose to go back." Ivy looked at Leander.

He took a moment to think. "I'm not sure." Oh but he was sure. Madison. His head pounded. Madison. Madison. Madison.

"You sure?" She said curiously, bringing him back to earth.

"Yep," He stood up out of the chair slowly and began cooking something on the stove, "Nothing to worry about."

She didn't answer. Not because she was mad. But because Leander had never acted like that before.

"How would we find it out?"

He spaced out.

"Leander."

"What?"

Ivy stood up from the chair and walked over to the stove where Leander was cooking. "How would we find out how I would get home?"

"There's no reason you have to go home, you know. You could just live in the forest with me."

"But I really want to go home. My mom is probably worried sick."

He sighed.

"What?"

"Hm?" He asked, looking at her.

"Why'd you sigh?"

He hesitated before answering. "I have to breathe to live." He laughed.

She gave an unamusing look.

He quickly stopped laughing. "Sorry. I didn't know I couldn't breathe around here."

She slumped down, "I'm sorry. I didn't mean to make you feel that way."

He didn't answer.

She felt horrible.

There was an awkward silence for a couple minutes. "Sorry Ivy. I sighed only because I don't want you to leave."

She seemed shocked. "It's okay, Leander."

"No, It's not." He tucked her hair behind her ear and hugged her tightly. She felt safe in his embrace. "Let's find out how to get you home." He opened his phone and quickly called Madison.

Before he could dial, Ivy swiftly took the phone out of his hand. Of course, she dropped it and it fell on the floor. She held her hands to her mouth, whispering, "I am so sorry."

"Don't worry about it. This baby has survived many drops." He said, picking it up.

She giggled.

"So what were you trying to say?" He snickered.

"Oh, I was going to say that I still don't know if I want to leave yet." She examined the ground.

Ivy? Stay here? With me? Wow, that would be great. Although I would need to keep up the act of being super funny and confident for a while. He thought it would be a great idea–

other than the thought of not being funny, of course.

"So? What do you think I should do?"

"Oh…um, I'm not sure," He mumbled.

She leaned her forearms on the cold countertop and positioned her hands on her chin. "What if we find out how I get home. Then I can choose whether or not I'm willing."

He took a moment to answer. He pretended he was thinking but instead, he was gazing at Ivy. "Sure, that works," he smiled.

She smiled back and slowly walked towards the door. He was still resting on the counter. Open the door for her. He walked quickly and opened the door before she could touch the door knob.

"Thank you," She chuckled.

As they walked closer to the castle, she would occasionally pick out some rocks or pebbles. Some were pink, some blue, some even neon green. He would frequently glance over at Ivy and help her collect rocks. "Have you ever tried to collect bark?" He asked. "They are pretty neat around here."

"Bark? Like tree bark?" she questioned, picking up more pebbles.

Leander nodded. "Mmm. Look." He took some bark out of his pocket and rubbed it gently.

Her eyes grew wide. "How? How could that even be possible?"

Leander shrugged and gave the–now purple–bark to Ivy. "I'm the only one who can do it."

"And you never told me that you could change bark colors? Leander, that's awesome!" She exclaimed as she gave it back.

He smiled at her as he placed it in his pocket once again. "No one has ever thought that it was that cool."

She looked up at him. "I do." She faced forward again, realizing she almost ran into a tree.

When they reached the castle, Leander led her upstairs to the round room where Madison was, situated on a wooden chair. Ivy would get weird looks–given that it seemed she was laying her arm out and had a ghost pulling her.

Leander, now out of breath, barged into the room. "Madison," he pulled Ivy closer.

"Yes?" she said, evidently annoyed.

"Get off of that type writer. I need your help."

"I don't take orders."

He was still holding Ivy's wrist. "Fine but we need to know how she gets home." He said, pointing at Ivy subtly.

She sat and thought for a moment. "Why?"

"You want her to leave, do you?" He whispered loud enough to where Ivy could hear what he was saying. She rolled her eyes.

"Okay. I'll find a way." She said as she gathered a couple pens and plopped them in a jar.

"How soon?"

"Soon enough."

He nodded and left, holding Ivy's wrist.

On the way out, Ivy asked, "What does soon enough mean?"

"Coming from her? Usually she already knows a way. She just wants us to wait."

Ivy stopped in her tracks. "I need to know now."

He stopped with her. "Ivy. you don't even know if you want to go home yet," he began walking slowly, "right?"

She accompanied him gradually and took a moment to answer. "Right." She replied.

He sat on a big rock beside a lake. "So, how are you going to choose?" He asked, looking at her from above.

"I don't know." She sighed and settled on a rock beside Leander.

Minutes passed. Together gazing at the astonishing view of the lake. "Ruisseau blanc." He mumbled.

"What?"

He looked at her. "That's the name of the

lake. It's French y'know."

"What does it mean?"

"White creek. It symbolizes all of the people in Eversect. Every citizen has a special rock. You get it when you're born. It kind of shows what you are going to turn out to be, I guess."

Her jaw was dangling. "Let's see yours."

He laughed sarcastically, "I'm not real. I don't have one. You do."

Her mouth, still open, practically drooling. "Why do I have one but you don't? I'm not necessarily a citizen."

He stumbled closer to the water. "Oh, but you are. You're forgetting that you're the Water Queen. I have always wondered who you were."

She followed him over the rocks and down to the lake. "So, what does that mean for you?"

"I've never known." He tried to change the topic, "Here's yours." He grasped it tightly. The rock was purple and smooth. It looked like it had been painted.

Ivy couldn't get any words out. "Mine? What does it say?"

Leander didn't say anything. All he did was grip onto it tighter. All Ivy could do was stand there. Tears grew in his eyes.

"Leander, what's wrong?" She asked as she walked closer to him, gently rubbing his shoulder.

"I've wanted to meet you for a while now." His voice cracked.

She could feel her chest ache. "Awe Leander." She tightly hugged him.

Seconds, maybe minutes passed by, still hugging as tight as they possibly could. He broke the hug and wiped his tears using his sleeve. "There are so many things I have wanted to tell you, but my heart breaks every time because I can't. I'm sorry."

"Leander, why can't you tell me?"

He shrugged.

She made an amused face and took his wrist. "Let's go back to the cottage and talk about what I'm going to do. Okay?"

He nodded slightly.

When they got there, they accompanied each other on the couch. Rain was pouring down and silence filled the lighting-lit room. Silently, Leander sat up and turned on the fan light.

Heavy breathing came from Ivy. While he was making his way back to the couch, she announced, "I want to go home."

He didn't say a word. He didn't even look at her. "I want you to stay with me." He slowly glanced over. "But my dad had always told me to never give me something I want." He fiddled with the bottom of his black shirt.

"Why would he say that?"

He looked up and gaped at the television screen. "I'm not sure. But I never want to get my way anyway. It always gives me something to lose."

She grasped her chest and hugged him. It was a bear-like hug. It was warm and affectionate, but also stiff at the same time. She felt safe but also awkward. While he was holding back tears.

Ivy broke the hug and wiped away his tears with her thumb. He briefly leaned on her hand gently. Leander looked in her eyes with a helpless look.

"Leander, why are you so sad?" She muttered, tears forming on the bottom eyelashes of her eyes.

"I don't want you to leave." He observed the tv to his left–trying his best not to look at her– making him cry more. He never liked showing his sensitive side. He had never had someone see him cry in his entire life. Except for his mom–of course.

She pouted. Ivy didn't know what to say. She could barely hold her tears back. "I want to stay."

"No, you don't."

She was speechless.

"You want to go home to your family. And that's okay." He grinned as he looked up at her. "I'll wait."

"For what?"

He laughed under his breath, "For you, Ivy."

She raised her eyebrows a bit, surprised anyone would wait for her.

Leander had never been into the whole "romance" thing. But she was different. She was kind and courageous. Beautiful and strong.

Eight
Let's Disappoint Each Other

Morning approached and Madison was already stirring some sort of mixture. Nobody else was in the castle but her. She liked being alone with her thoughts. She never liked the idea of someone getting in the way or messing up her magnificent plan. She heard someone nearing the kitchen where she was.

"You're up early," A voice echoed.

She rolled her eyes. "Yes, Lord. My job."

He poured himself a cup of coffee and sipped it while leaning on the countertop next to Madison. She tensed her lips in annoyance. This was her only time in the entire day she got to be alone, and he ruined it. She threw her mixing spoon on the counter and headed to the large freezer in the back–the only freezer in the forest that carries potions–she opened it and grabbed the first thing she saw, hoping the Lord would take a hint to leave.

"Got a lot to do today?" He asked casually. She hated when he asked a bunch of unreasonable questions in the morning.

"Yeah. You?"

"I'm the Lord, Madison. Respect me. I may be your father but there is no reason for any attitude around here."

She rolled her eyes yet again as she placed dishes in the sink and began scrubbing harshly. "I just don't understand why Ivy of all people gets to be the Water Queen. I'm the princess.

He put his coffee mug down and paced to the other room. "You don't understand, child, no one can know that you are my daughter," he shouted.

She walked into the opposite room of the Lord and folded some laundry. "Yes but why?"

He rolled his eyes. Madison didn't repeat the question. She was too scared he would yell. Again.

Madison drew her attention to the big wooden doors opening from the front of the castle. She figured it was Fonic, given that he was the only one who ever actually showed up on time.

And there he went, clipboard in hand, already writing something down with his small pen. "Morning Madison." He said, not looking up from his clipboard and snatching the Lord's coffee off of the countertop.

"Good morning Fonic." She muttered, also not taking an eye off of the laundry she was folding.

Madison finally had a bit of free time. She decided to rest on the couch in the living room, patiently waiting for Leander. He's always late. All because of Ivy. They have a weird connection. I hate it.

She opened her book, glancing behind her to the window outside. Madison never liked reading. She had always thought it was boring. But he seemed to like girls who read and who are quiet, so she tried her best.

Finally, she saw Leander's shadow peeking from around the corner. She made sure to situate herself on the couch nicely. But when he turned to come inside, she saw Ivy with him. She pursed her lips in an angry way.

When they walked in together, they were laughing. But when they saw Madison, they stopped. She tried her best to pretend she didn't see them, but couldn't help herself. All she had to do was become close friends with them. Then, it would all be over. She stood up from the couch, closed her book, and ran over to Ivy. They hugged and said their "hello's." She awkwardly side-hugged Leander. Making sure to say good morning and be polite.

"Do you guys want to hang sometime?" Madison walked with them nervously. Trying her best to play it cool.

"Hang?" Leander chuckled.

"Yeah. Like a hangout."

Ivy giggled.

"What's so funny?"

"Oh, nothing saying 'hang' was just…different I guess."

She perched an eyebrow and crossed her arms.

Leander and Ivy, both exchanging looks to each other. Leander's look saying: "why is she acting so weird?"

And Ivy's saying: "Who knows."

"Well? Do you guys want to…"

"Hang?" Leander finished her sentence and smiled.

Madison was slightly annoyed that he was mocking her but also happy that he was actually talking to her.

Leander laughed again as he answered, "Sure. When and where?"

Ivy nudged his shoulder, and Madison could tell she was jealous. So, she tried to make her more jealous.

"Maybe we could chill by the lake? Just me and you?" She smirked.

Ivy glared at Leander as Madison's smirk

grew bigger and bigger. He examined the ground, "Why can't Ivy come with?"

"Honestly, what did I ever do?" Ivy asked loudly.

Madison flung her arms in the air, like she was surrendering to the police, "Whoa, Whoa, Whoa, I just want some quality time with my best friend." She declared, still smirking.

Ivy rolled her eyes as Leander peered behind him to look at her. He could tell that she was jealous so he grabbed Ivy's wrist and tensely said, "no thanks, I'm good."

Madison's smile faded as she backed up a step. "Fine. I was only told to hang out with you anyway." She walked speedily upstairs to her room. She overheard them laughing in the background.

She entered her room and immediately flopped on her pink, silk bed sheets and began crying. Black mascara soaked the pillow case as she wrapped her arms around the blanket she always folded specially for herself. Why her? Why not me? What did I do? She thought.

She heard loud footsteps coming up the stairs. "Madison! Stop messing around and get to work! These potions aren't going to mix themselves!"

She quickly wiped her tears, got up and pretended she was dusting the entire time.

"Oh, it's clean here." He said as soon as he barged in Madison's room.

She nodded. "What do you need?" She spoke as she tried wiping away her tears secretively.

"I need you to get to work. Now." He ordered as he strutted out of the door.

Madison was still holding back tears, as long as "dusting."

After a couple minutes, she decided to finally go downstairs and get to work. She would have to do it; sad or not.

Walking down the stairs, she could see a sliver of Leander and Ivy sitting on the couches. Laughing and talking as usual. She pretended not to see them and kept walking toward the mixing room.

She flicked on the light and headed toward the table where she had been working on special dust yesterday. She sat down and took the small lid off of the mason jar that was holding the strange dust. Madison knew what it was. But no one else could ever know. She began mixing with a small stirring spoon. Small enough to where a dwarf could even carry it.

Their laughs were pounding in Madison's head. She tried so hard to discard it. Madison realized she had to carry the dust out to the kitchen for testing. But she would have to walk right past Leander and Ivy.

Maybe this dust will make them question and they will have come up to me.

She tried her best to keep her eyes on the dust, gradually placing droplets in it. Out of the corner of her eye, she could view them sitting up from their seats, walking closer and closer to Madison.

"Whoa, Madison, what is this?" Ivy ran up to her and cupped the bottom of the mason jar, making Madison pull it away.

"Things."

Ivy started to turn the mason jar to look at the label written on the side of it before Madison quickly jolted it back to where it was. "You'll find out soon." She said quietly as she walked away slowly.

"How soon?" Ivy followed.

Madison took a glance at Leander, who was still sitting on the couch, reading a book. He already knew that the jar held the memories. She ignored Ivy and tramped out of the room to the kitchen.

She entered and slammed the door, making sure to lock it. Madison smacked the jar of memories on the table, graciously taking out the small cup of love from the front pocket of her apron. She took off the lid of the memories and quickly transferred them to the jar of love. She took her small stirring spoon and began mixing them together as fast as she could.

The Lord would be furious If he found out that she was late to mixing them. And she knew it. This would be the number one thing to take over Eversect and she couldn't ruin it.

How would this dust take over Eversect you ask? Well, it will first put everyone to sleep. Then, all of the trees will start dying. Next, everyone should wake up after three days. Madison will eventually become the queen. And according to her plan, the Lord may die.

All she had to do was put the dust in a machine during the last blood moon of the year. Which was tomorrow night. The trick was to place it just right on a scepter. But not just any scepter.

Cosmo's scepter.

The most powerful scepter of all time. I mean, it keeps all of the love in the entire forest.

Madison grew a large smirk just thinking about it. She was so thrilled she would finally become the queen of Eversect. She liked that name.

The next day finally came and Madison was ready. She got up early and jolted downstairs. She was determined to become queen today.

Madison headed for the kitchen as fast as

she could, almost bumping into three dwarves on her way. She heard the Lord's footsteps. She would normally be nervous about what he was going to say next. But today was the day. She didn't care.

But Madison stopped in her tracks when she saw Leander out of the corner of her eye. He was alone this time. So, what did Madison do, you ask? She ran up to him and gave him a huge hug, exclaiming, "Leander! Today is the day! Today is the day that we get to take over Eversect!" She saw his smile fade as he cupped her hands in his. "What's wrong?" She asked with a slight head tilt.

He looked down at his feet, letting go of her hands. "I forgot we were doing that today."

"Why are you so sad about it?" Her face stiffened.

He quickly looked up at her and fixed his posture. "Oh, sorry, I'm not. Just tired."

She slightly squinted her eyes. She would normally blow up on him but today was an exciting day. "So where's Ivy?"

"You ordered me to come alone. So I did. She's at my cottage."

Madison nodded her head with a smile. "Great." Madison walked over to the kitchen again, leading Leander by holding his hand.

She brought him over to the table where the

dust and where the scepter was. She held the scepter gently and revealed it to Leander.

"Wow." He said, his eyes wide, taking it with one hand.

Her face lit up, hearing reassurance from him. He likes it. That's all that matters.

"How did you even get a hold of this?"

"It wasn't easy given that they are home now. We had one of the dark unicorns get into their yard and eat their flowers," she chuckled.

He laughed and high-fived her. "So what time are we doing this?" He put his hands in his front pockets.

"Exactly 10pm tonight"

He took a moment to answer, gaping at her eyes. "Sure."

She smiled brightly. "Let's get it ready then."

"Great. How can I help?"

"You can start by putting the dust in that special bottle. We will connect it to the scepter when it's time."

"Sounds good."

A couple minutes went by with complete silence. Madison was concentrating intently, stirring the dust constantly to make sure the dust wouldn't form any lumps.

Leander was carefully examining the scepter. He had always been into stuff like this. Cool antiques, potions, but most of all, the evilness that came with all of it. A devilish smirk appeared on his face. Worse than Madison's. "This is so exciting." He mentioned, placing the scepter on the table once again.

She laughed as she put more water droplets in the dust. "I'm like 75% sure this won't explode."

He looked over to her speedily and giggled.

"I have an awkward question for you." Madison always liked to address when she felt awkward or if she was about to be.

"Yeah?"

"Are you and Ivy…I don't know…a thing?" She asked as slow as she possibly could.

"Me and Ivy? Oh I'm not sure. I think she likes me."

Madison's face dropped. "Do you like her?" That question made her stomach in knots.

"Maybe." He didn't take an eye off of the ground after he sat on the chair closest to the table.

She got nervous. It felt as though her heart had been punctured a million times over by a million tiny pins.

"But I might not ever have a shot with her anyway."

"Yeah?" She finally felt hope return in her sunken chest.

He frowned. "I guess."

She shrugged her shoulders in embarrassment.

He shoved her shoulder lightly as she grinned, "Where did that dust even come from anyway?"

She held it up a little bit, for him to get a better sight of it, "obviously from Fawn and Cosmo. But I think they got it from the sky somewhere." Madison set it down. She thought about how nice it was that Ivy wasn't getting in the way of her time with her Leander.

He paused. "The sky? How?"

She sat down next to him and crossed her legs nicely, "you know Cosmo can fly, right? He probably got it somewhere," Before he could answer, she shot up from her chair, "unless…" she walked as fast as she could.

Leander stood up as well and slowly followed. "Unless…?"

She squatted and opened a cabinet closest to the floor. Madison removed a large manual and instantly began reading the table of contents.

"Unless what?!" Leander exclaimed.

She still didn't answer. She was too concentrated. Madison flipped to the page she needed, titled:

Strange Dust; the only guide you'll ever need!

She swiftly read through, licking her fingertip every time she needed to flip a page. Leander slouched back in his chair, knowing better not to ask what she was doing. Again.

"Where does dust come from?" She read the heading aloud, "here we go," She shared the book with Leander, "some say it's a myth, blah, blah, blah," she mumbled, skipping over the words, "Fawn and Cosmo are founders, yeah, yeah, yeah," her eyes skimmed the page, searching for an answer as to where she's seen the weird dust before.

"What are you even looking for? Plus, it's getting late and I told Ivy I would be back by eleven."

"That doesn't matter. She'll assume you're at work." She flipped through more pages.

"You didn't answer my question." He said sternly.

"Well then ask it again and I might answer this time. That's how it works." She raised her eyebrows, not taking an eye off of her manual.

"Or you could just answer it the first time," he announced quite loudly.

She rolled her eyes yet again, "please just repeat the question. It won't kill you."

He closed his eyes and took a deep breath, "I was wondering what you are even looking for."

"I'm trying to find where I've seen this dust before."

"You've seen this before?" He asked, holding the small jar up, "the only magical dust in the entire forest?" He examined it intensely, he brought it as close as he could to his eyes.

Madison snatched it back from him and held it close to her chest, "yes, and I would like for it to stay in one piece until 10 tonight–at least."

He nodded.

Madison studied the manual again. She began mumbling, "Some say it's in the sky," she glared at the book, "who doesn't know that?" She sighed and kept reading.

Leander let out a big yawn and stretched his arms back. "Well I'm going to make some coffee while you're figuring this out."

She stopped reading for a moment, "coffee? At 9:30? Good luck with that." She drew her attention back toward the book.

He didn't answer.

"Found it!" She hollered. "The dust originated from a shed," her eyes grew wider than they've ever been in her entire life before, "shed?" She read faster, "from–specifically– the Water Queen's backyard." She whispered.

Leander happened to be walking in at that exact moment. "Water Queen? Like, Ivy?"

Madison's heartbeat increased but she tried her best not to show it. "Yeah it looks like it."

"What's wrong? You seem tense." He set his

coffee down as he took his seat on his regular chair.

She came back to earth, "Me? Nope, I'm great."

He began eating something he must have picked up in the kitchen. "How did you know that the Lord was your dad? Y'know, since you came from 'far, far away' and what not."

She took a moment to think, "I guess I realized that I never had a father figure in my life, and well, when I met him, we kind of just clicked. So I asked him and he finally realized that I was his daughter. I never knew how that worked, though, given that…um, nevermind."

He took another bite and chewed loudly, shrugging his shoulders.

She spaced out again and thought really hard about what the amnual had said.

Shed. The shed Ivy and I came into in the first place. I wish we were still close friends. This is the dust. This is the dust that started it all. I can't believe that I'm actually doing this. She thought. "Hey it's getting to be 9:50, we should get ready for the blood moon." Madison tried to distract herself.

All he did was nod.

It began to get closer to 10 o'clock and Leander was having second thoughts. "Are you sure we should do this Madison? It seems like a lot of work just for you to be queen don't ya' think?"

"You're just being lazy, this will work." She replied, making sure every last detail was in place.

"Please just let it go. We can find a way for you to be queen a different way. I promise." He was desperate. He didn't want everyone to get put to sleep.

She hesitated. "Leander you don't understand. This means so much."

He didn't have any words left in his body. He zoned out and thought about everything that may happen and how to talk her out of it. "Madison, stop."

She ignored him.

"Madison."

"Leander." She refused to look at him.

He tried to think of something he could possibly say to distract her, "you like me right?"

"What? How do you know? Not that I do or anything. But how'd you find out?"

"I took a guess," he took her hands, "Madison, if you don't do this, we can be together, as long as we live. Please, you don't have to be queen." His voice cracked.

Madison really wanted to be queen. But if this was her chance to be with Leander, she had to take it. "Fine." She kicked the scepter down, wrapping her arms around him.

Tears filled in his eyes. He knew he didn't want this, but it was what had to be done. He kept thinking about how upset Ivy would be when she found out. He really hated being with Madison.

While Madison was in heaven hugging the man of her dreams. She was the only girl he wanted. She was the only one he would ever date.

Leander finally broke the hug, saying "I should get back home."

"Oh," her voice cracked, "I thought maybe you could stay with me for a little? Since we're a 'thing' now." She smiled.

"I want to go back home now." He said awkwardly, plucking his coat off of the coat rack.

Madison relaxed her shoulders, not knowing what was going on with him. She really wanted to be with him. And she thought he did too.

He slammed the door and Madison went upstairs to her room again and began crying. She just wanted someone to actually care for her. She had never had a lot of friends except for Ivy and Leander. And now that might've been gone too. She hated every second of it.

Leander walked right into the cottage where

he found Ivy sleeping on the couch with the blue blanket he lended her a couple days ago. The television was on, playing a movie Leander didn't recognize. He sat his coat and keys down on the countertop and made his way to a recliner chair he had next to the couch. He observed the movie playing.

Ivy must have caught him sitting down. She woke up and peered over at him. "Hey." She mumbled, turning over on her back to get a better view of where he was.

"Hey," he smiled.

"What were you doing at work? It's 11:30 already."

"Yeah. Just had a lot of catching up to do I guess." She shrugged.

She sat up and wrapped the blanket around her shoulders. "We both know that's not true."

He tried not to make anything obvious but he failed. He ended up telling her everything that had happened–not including getting with Madison.

"That sounds so bad. Did you even want to do it?" she asked, trying her best to sound nonchalant.

"Kinda. But not to be a bad person or anything."

Ivy didn't want to tear him down so all she did was nod politely. He knew how much being in the court meant to him. She didn't want to ruin that.

"Ivy, I want to tell you something. But you can't freak out. Okay?"

"Depends on what it is." She crossed her arms and raised an eyebrow in a joking manner.

He didn't even giggle, "this is serious."

Ivy didn't want to say anything else.

He took a second to get it out, but eventually, he spoke, "I am with Madison."

She ignored the sentence and pretended not to understand. She felt her heart drop, "of course you are, you're with her every day for work." She managed to put a fake smile on her face, making it harder for him to explain.

"No, Ivy, I'm actually with her, meaning, like, dating." Leander couldn't believe he actually said that out loud.

Her eyebrows rose in an unusual way. She felt her heart throb as tears swelled up in her eyes.

Leander took her hand, "let me explain,"

She was speechless.

"Please."

She looked up at him with tears in her eyes. "No." She forced her hand back aggressively and ran out the door."

"It's too dark out there for you to be alone." He shouted to nothing but air. He was alone in

his own house. And he knew he ruined everything.

Nine
Nasty, Dirty, Brutal

Ivy was sitting outside on her usual rock and gaping at the sunrise over the trees and hills. Why would he do this? I thought he liked me. She wanted to hear him explain but not right now, she couldn't even look at him. She thought it was disgusting. There is no way this is real. She plugged in her headphones and took a walk around the forest as she always seemed to do.

Leander felt terrible. He didn't like to see her in pain–especially when he was the one who made her that way. He poured himself a glass of wine that was sitting out on the counter from the night before. He remembered to not offer Ivy any because;

1.   She was mad–obviously.
2.   She was only eighteen.

He felt relieved as well, though. Now the secret was out and he didn't have to stress about telling her. He really liked Ivy though.

He never thought anything would ever happen between him and Madison. Leander hadn't thought about it.

He was just glad that Madison didn't do anything with the dust. But now he had to figure out how to get it back to Fawn and Cosmo without them knowing they ever took it.

He decided to talk to Ivy about it. (Yes, he should be talking to Madison about it, but no, he's a boy.) So, he quickly escaped his front door and sprinted to Ivy.

Once he found her sitting on the other side of Ruisseau Blanc, he sat down with her in silence. Crickets chirped in the background. Leander rested his hand on her knee but she lifted it out of reach for him to try. This isn't going to go well, he thought.

"Leander," she muttered, "I really liked you. And I thought you liked me. I really did. I guess I was just being foolish."

He stared down at the rocks below them, "I do, Ivy."

"No, you don't. You're dating her."

"I didn't know what else to do. She was going to put everyone to sleep with the dust you collected. She was going to use it to turn against everyone and become queen. I made the stupid suggestion that we could date if she didn't do it. I never meant to hurt you."

She wouldn't believe him at first. Ivy didn't even want to reply. But she forced words out of herself. "No way."

He relaxed his shoulders a bit to her response, "yeah, I really don't like her. But I really like you."

Her heart ran fast as her breathing sped up. "Really?"

"Yes, really."

She smiled brightly.

"I need to talk to Madison about this, I promise everything will work out. Promise."

Ivy held her pinky out, proposing a pinky promise.

He took it tightly.

The next morning arrived and Leander was the first one to get up in the morning. She woke up and walked downstairs to a delicious smelling breakfast. "Good morning," she said with a yawn.

"Morning." He answered, flipping a pancake. "I'm going down to the castle today," he announced.

"But it's Saturday. I was thinking we could hang out today." She announced as she sat on the bar stools

"You're forgetting about 'the thing' I have to talk to Madison about."

She gave him a slight nod, taking a sip of her coffee.

Before anyone could speak again, a dwarf barged into Leander's cottage, shouting, "Guys! Guys! I have terrible, beyond terrible news for you!"

Leander walked closer to the dwarf and Ivy followed. "What happened?" He asked intriguingly.

The small dwarf took a moment to catch his breath, hands on his knees. He held his hand in the air, holding up a number one, to signal them to give him a minute.

Ivy grabbed his shoulders tightly. "What is it?!" She hollered.

The dwarf held his hands half way in the air. "Gimme a minute, gimme a minute!" He shouted.

"If you would tell us what it is, she wouldn't have grabbed you." Leander raised his eyebrows and leaned on the wall, hands in his pockets.

"Alright, alright," he raised his hands again, "I have terrible news...about Madison." He folded his hands and hung his head.

"What?" She dropped the pen she was fidgeting with moments before, "what happened?" Madison may have done awful things, but she was still Ivy's best friend in the whole wide world.

Leander rested his hand on her shoulder in worry.

"I'm afraid Madison has run away. No one knows where, all we know is that she used the special dust somehow. We found out she was under some evil spell by the Lord. I am so sorry."

Leander could see Ivy about to break down so to be respectful, he made sure to ask the dwarf to excuse them.

She broke down on the floor. She had already felt this heart wrenching feeling before. But this time it was real. This time she wasn't going to come back. Ivy didn't know what to do but cry. She might be dead. She thought.

When the evening passed, both Leander and Ivy were sitting on the couch watching a movie. Her cheeks were coated with mascara. Leander had lent her his favorite sweatshirt to make sure she was comfortable. She ended up falling asleep on his shoulder. And he looked down at her every once-in-a-while to make sure she was still sleeping peacefully, gliding his pinky finger down the border of her nose.

*****

You might be wondering how I know all of these things, well, that's because I experienced them.

After all, I am the one and only, Ivy.

In case you were wondering . . .

In the end, Leander and Ivy ended up together once and for all. Ivy made the decision to stay in the forest and rule forever with Leander by her side as the king.
Don't worry about her parents, they visit often :)

Oh, I almost forgot, the dust and the scepter were used by Madison to get back home–England to be specific–mostly because she missed her parents. Madison became good. And everything worked out. Her and Ivy became closer friends than before.

(This may or may not be...)
THE END

About the Author

Jolene Rose (that's a pen-name, by the way) wrote Ivy Jones' Incredible Adventure at age twelve. It is her first book. She lives in Colorado.

9 781954 518117